MISSING LIVES

A DETECTIVE CHARLOTTE PIERCE MYSTERY

LAST BREATH
BOOK 4

KATE GABLE

COPYRIGHT

C opyright © 2022 by Byrd Books, LLC.
All rights reserved.

Editor: Kevin Doran

Proofreaders:

Julie Deaton, Deaton Author Services, https://www.facebook.com/jdproofs/

Renee Waring, Guardian Proofreading Services, https://www.facebook.com/GuardianProofreadingServices

Cover Design: Kate Gable

Visit my website at www.kategable.com

BE THE FIRST TO KNOW ABOUT MY UPCOMING SALES, NEW RELEASES AND EXCLUSIVE GIVEAWAYS!

W ant a Free book? Sign up for my Newsletter!

Sign up for my newsletter:

https://www.subscribepage.com/kategableviplist

Join my Facebook Group:
https://www.facebook.com/groups/833851020557518

Bonus Points: Follow me on BookBub and
Goodreads!

https://www.goodreads.com/author/show/21534224.
Kate_Gable

ABOUT KATE GABLE

Kate Gable loves a good mystery that is full of suspense. She grew up devouring psychological thrillers and crime novels as well as movies, tv shows and true crime.

Her favorite stories are the ones that are centered on families with lots of secrets and lies as well as many twists and turns. Her novels have elements of psychological suspense, thriller, mystery and romance.

Kate Gable lives near Palm Springs, CA with her husband, son, a dog and a cat. She has spent more than twenty years in Southern California and finds inspiration from its cities, canyons, deserts, and small mountain towns.

She graduated from University of Southern California with a Bachelor's degree in Mathematics. After pursuing graduate studies in mathematics, she switched gears and got her MA in Creative Writing and English from Western New Mexico University and her PhD in Education from Old Dominion University.

Writing has always been her passion and obsession. Kate is also a USA Today Bestselling author of romantic suspense under another pen name.

Write her here:

Kate@kategable.com

Check out her books here:

www.kategable.com

Sign up for my newsletter:
https://www.subscribepage.com/kategableviplist

Join my Facebook Group:
https://www.facebook.com/groups/833851020557518

Bonus Points: Follow me on BookBub and Goodreads!

https://www.bookbub.com/authors/kate-gable

https://www.goodreads.com/author/show/21534224.Kate_Gable

ALSO BY KATE GABLE

All books are available at ALL major retailers! If you can't find it, please email me at
kate@kategable.com
www.kategable.com

Detective Kaitlyn Carr

Girl Missing (Book 1)
Girl Lost (Book 2)
Girl Found (Book 3)
Girl Taken (Book 4)
Girl Forgotten (Book 5)

Girl Hidden (FREE Novella)

Detective Charlotte Pierce

Last Breath
Nameless Girl
Missing Lives
Girl in the Lake

Lake of Lies (FREE Novella)

ABOUT MISSING LIVES

☆☆☆☆☆ "The twists come at you at breakneck pace. Very suspenseful." (Goodreads)

When two young boys disappear while riding their bikes, Detective Charlotte Pierce must follow the clues to find their killer before he strikes again.

In the dusty outskirts of Mesquite County, California, two kids go missing, taken from outside their homes. The quiet desert community is devastated and it's up to Charlotte to find out what happened.

The FBI is called in and a man who stalked and terrorized Charlotte comes back into her life. She kept his secret to protect her career, but is now being forced to work with him to solve the case.

What happens when she confronts him about what he has done? What happens when the killer start searching for another victim?

This suspenseful thriller is perfect for fans of James Patterson, Leslie Wolfe, Lisa Regan, L. T. Vargus and Karin Slaughter. It has mystery, angst, a bit of romance and family drama.

Praise for Kate Gable's Girl Missing Series

⭐⭐⭐⭐⭐"Gripping! This book was a great read. I found a new author that I enjoy and I can't wait to read the rest of the series! " *(Goodreads)*

⭐⭐⭐⭐⭐ "The twists come at you at breakneck pace. Very suspenseful." *(Goodreads)*

⭐⭐⭐⭐⭐ "I really enjoyed the ins and outs of the storyline, it kept me reading so that I could find out how the story would turn out. And the ending was a major shocker, I never saw it coming. I truly recommend this book to everyone who loves mysteries and detective stories." *(Goodreads)*

⭐⭐⭐⭐⭐" I loved it. One of the best books I've ever read." - Amazon review

⭐⭐⭐⭐⭐ "I couldn't put the book down I give it a thumbs up and I would recommend it to other readers" *(Goodreads)*

★★★★★ "Another great book in the Kaitlyn Carr series! I am so drawn into these books. I love that they are not just about Kaitlyn's search for her sister but also about a case she is working on. I can't wait for the final book in the series!" *(Goodreads)*

1

KELSEY

I haven't known the girls for long and was pleasantly surprised when they invited me to the concert. I've been trying hard to cover up just how much I don't like living in Long Beach and how much I miss Seattle.

The rainy days. The drizzle. The better music scene.

But Charlotte, Clara, Stephanie, and Briana have gone out of their way to make me feel welcome here, and I appreciate that more than I can say.

The whole sarcastic attitude of me being cooler than everyone else because I am from Seattle is more of an act than anything else. A shield, a way to protect myself from the mistakes that I've made, and the regrets that I have.

My parents fight nonstop, almost like it's a second job. The few times that I brought up the idea of them going to counseling, they laughed. They didn't really care that I didn't want to move, but I had to leave all my friends. They said that it'd be healthy for me to meet new people but the truth is that my dad got a job at Cal State Long Beach and they moved because of money.

It's a reality of the situation besides the fact that it's much cheaper here, and the salary goes further, but it's not like we do anything as a family anyway.

Mom spends way too much time drinking in the afternoons because she had to leave her job behind, and Dad is busy in the office. One of the reasons they moved and something they don't know that I know is that Dad had a girlfriend.

His student. How banal is that? So pathetic. It makes me want to throw up.

Mom found out about it. Made a big stink at the university. Got him fired essentially, and the student broke up with him.

I guess Mom got what she wanted, but at what price? I would have dumped him immediately. I talked to her about it but she told me that I was a little girl who didn't understand. What I don't understand is letting some man walk all over you like this.

Mom had a good job in Seattle; she was a buyer for Nordstrom. She liked it. Fashion was something that she was interested in. What is she doing here? Nothing of substance. Just drinking the days away.

Mom has no friends, no interests, nothing, and we've been here for months. I hate going home and I hate seeing her that way, buzzed with the TV on constantly. Barely showering.

She thinks that Dad won't have another affair, but who can be around her now? There's nothing fun about her. All the spark is gone.

IT WASN'T that long ago that I admired my mom. I loved spending time with her. Going out to lunch, trying on clothes. I wanted her approval of my thrift store finds because she wasn't just some Nordstrom snob. She had a real flair for fashion.

When she was younger, she even wanted to open a boutique and design her own clothing line, but she hitched her star to my father. All of these years later, he just cast her aside. But worse than that, she went crawling after him, begging him to stay, forcing him out of his job, and moving us here.

Dad acts like he doesn't resent her, but we all know that he does. If his girlfriend hadn't broken up with him, they'd probably be married by now, but she cheated on him just like he cheated on my mom.

Don't you just love that kind of irony? Here I am, thirteen, going to a strange school with strange friends who care nothing about the music and the fashion that I like. I have to meet them where they are, share their interests because otherwise I'll have no one and the days are just too long to spend by yourself.

The concert is Clara's idea. It's a popular band in a big arena and not my scene at all, but I pretend I like it as I try to introduce my new group of friends to some of the cool things that I like to listen to.

"Your clothes have definitely changed since you moved down here. So much black now," Mom says, walking into my room. "You still haven't unpacked your boxes or put up all of your posters. Do you need help with that?"

She tries to get her crap together every afternoon. I know that she has been frantically cleaning the house. I doubt that it was for longer than twenty minutes but she still seems exhausted.

Everything makes her exhausted.

"I just don't feel like unpacking quite yet," I say.

"You know that you're staying here, right?" Mom sits on the edge of my bed.

My poster boards of collages are still propped up against the wall. I had cut photos out of magazines to express myself. It's something that I would later discover is called a vision board. But I didn't have a word for it quite yet. They sit against the wall, waiting to be hung up and loved and adored just like they were back home.

"I thought you would enjoy the ocean. It's so close," Mom continues to push. "You can ride your bike."

"Would you like to do that sometime?" I ask her.

She seems startled by the idea. "Yes, maybe, but I'm tired today."

"That's because you don't do anything, Mom," I say. My voice is filled with disappointment. "Dad is moving on with his life, so why can't you?"

"Dad has a job," she says.

"Exactly, what, there's no Nordstrom here? I'm sure you can get a transfer."

"I just don't know if I'm up for it, Kelsey. It has been a hard adjustment for me. If you remember, I was the one that packed everything, unpacked, and organized the move."

"Unpacked?" I ask. "The living room has more boxes than my room. I guess there's someone else who doesn't want to make this place a home."

"I think we should both try, Kelsey," Mom says.

I look at her in the mirror and see that she has gained at least twenty pounds since we got here. Her clothes don't fit right. She knows as well as I do, and she's embarrassed by this fact. That's probably why she doesn't want to be active or join a gym. Pilates was her go-to workout back home.

"I, at least, have friends," I say. "Why don't you do some pottery or go to yoga?"

"I don't feel like making friends." Mom shrugs. "And yoga's too early in the morning."

"There are ten o'clock classes at the local gym in Belmont Shore. You can walk there from here," I say.

That is the one thing I really enjoy about living here. In Seattle, we lived in more of a suburb where I needed to be driven everywhere, but here we are within walking distance of the water and Second Street. Belmont Shore makes me feel like a cool kid. I don't need rides. I can get around by myself. Luckily my parents let me bike wherever I want. There are also a number of thrift stores, even if they are ridiculously overpriced.

"I'm going to a sleepover tomorrow. Did I tell you?" I say, going along with a lie, even though the truth would probably be okay.

My friends' parents were categorically against the concert, but I doubt Mom would care that much. I don't bother asking however, since we all came up with this elaborate network of lies, where we're saying that we're sleeping over at different friends' houses.

Stephanie has the biggest problem. Charlotte's dad is hardly involved, though he seems adamant about certain rules and regulations that you follow, but Stephanie's mom is completely nuts. She doesn't even like the idea of her having friends, let alone being interested in boys.

What else does she think that a thirteen-year-old girl thinks about? School? Perhaps.

Stephanie is definitely good at that, but she has a crush on a guy in school in math class. They even made out already.

Liam spends most of his time surfing. In fact, hoping to be professional, and with the little time that's left, he skateboards. If I were to tell you what a Southern California kid would be, it would be him. He and Stephanie seem like an odd couple. He's not exactly stupid, but single-minded. Interested in surfing first, skateboarding second, and doing tricks on his BMX bike third.

But Liam's sweet and I can see why he and Stephanie hit it off when she tutored him. Plus, he's really hot, has tan skin, long blond hair, and bright blue eyes. At first, I thought it was a joke that he was into Stephanie. She's nerdy, with thick bottle-like lenses for glasses. She has a good sense of humor and she is really smart. I guess he fell for her over the quadratic equation.

The problem is that his parents basically have no rules and Stephanie has a million rules. So far, that has given their relationship something of a Romeo and Juliet quality. Raising the stakes of their romance, no doubt.

But what about when he gets sick of it? When he wants a girlfriend to just be able to go see him surf on a Saturday morning? Or go out to a movie Friday night? Stephanie isn't allowed to do any of those things.

We had already covered for her multiple times with her mom saying that she's spending time with us when she's really with Liam. What about later when he gets tired of that, at least that's what Clara says. She's dwelling on what's going to happen to their relationship because she's living vicariously through it. I knew she had a crush on Liam before Stephanie but never did anything about it and took a step back when they hooked up, but I know she's still jealous.

Liam is hot, and he doesn't seem to really know it. All the girls in school have a crush on him, but he has eyes only for Stephanie. Everyone seems to be just waiting for them to break up. It hasn't happened yet.

But when it does, I wonder what's going to become of our little clique?

Will we stay friends or will Clara pouncing on Stephanie's ex be too much?

Either way, I'm here for the drama.

2

KELSEY

"I'm really happy that you have friends here," Mom says. "Look, you're going to sleepovers! You have a nice little crew, don't you?"

"Yes," I say, doodling on a notebook, dressed in all black.

According to my previous version of Mom, my Seattle mom, dressing in black is boring. It's the easiest way to look sophisticated but it's also the least interesting.

My outfit today is anything but sophisticated. Ripped black jeans, Doc Martens boots, an oversized black t-shirt, and a bunch of black rubber bands around my wrists. I've been adding to my bracelet collection over some time alternating between leather, metal, and black bands for no other reason except that it makes me feel like I'm a cooler version of myself.

"I miss my old friends Didi and Tyler," I say with a sigh.

This is the most that I've opened up to my mom in a while.

"I know that, sweetie, but you seem to be having a better time here than I am."

"That's just because you don't have any friends and you're trying desperately to hold on to a man who doesn't love you," I say, a little bit under my breath.

"Don't talk to me like that," Mom snaps. "I may act like your friend but I'm still your mother and I can ground you and stop you from going to the sleepover."

"Why don't you?" I challenge her. "Why don't we go instead to Nordstrom? You can get all dressed up and get a job there. You can be your old self."

"Oh, honey, don't be silly."

"I know that you're nervous because you've gained some weight but you can lose it. I can help you."

Mom looks at me with a shocked expression on her face. Was she thinking that I didn't notice? Was she hoping that I knew nothing about it?

"Mom, I know you're not happy with Dad. Why are you even with him?"

"He and I are trying to move on. You know that."

"I know but there's no point. I mean, you're never going to forgive him."

"Of course, I will. I have. You don't understand the first thing about marriage or commitment and I hope that, for your sake, in the future, you give your husband some leeway to make mistakes."

"Is that what we're calling it now? Leeway? To just cheat? No, I'm not going to do that. It's not cool and it's not romantic. It's abusive and toxic. I'm thirteen years old and I know this, and you're my mother and you don't. I can still have a relationship with my dad but *you* don't have to. I know that he didn't cheat on me even though it sort of feels like he did. He can still be my dad but I don't know why you're putting up with any of it."

"Because I love him, Kelsey. Because I've been with him for years and I know who he is and I know what mistakes he made and what mistakes I made."

"What mistakes did *you* make?" I ask.

"You're my daughter and I'm not going to go into details like that."

"Why?" I get to the edge of the bed. "That's exactly who you need to tell all of these details to. I'm the one who has to understand these ridiculous decisions that you're making."

My mom gets up from my desk chair and looks out the window. There's a big oak tree outside swaying in the wind. It's sunny and the marine layer burned off earlier in the morning. I would hate to admit this to her but I like the weather here. You get a little bit of the gloom in the morning to start your day off, but in the afternoon it's sunny and bright and the beach is warm and happy and the water is blue.

"I'm just worried about you, Mom," I say. "I hate seeing you like this, sad and like you don't belong when really you belong in so many more places. There's so much more to you. I mean, I know that Dad has his work and he's busy with that. He's always been obsessed and kind of a workaholic, but I want you to get back to what you're passionate about, too. What you love to do. You used to be so happy. We can go thrifting. If you don't want to get your old job back, we can do something else. I just want to be with you, Mom, your old self."

"I can't be my old self, Kelsey." She shakes her head. "That person is gone."

"Why?" I ask. "Why can't you be your old self?"

"Because she died in Seattle," Mom says, turning around to face me.

There are tears in her eyes and one breaks free and rolls down her cheek. Her hair is up in a bun; she's wearing an oversized t-shirt and sweatpants. Sometimes she makes an effort after school but not today. Cleaning up was enough but she hasn't showered.

"I know you're depressed but you can get over it. You just have to try."

"That's not how depression works, Kelsey. It's a mental disorder. It just gets worse and worse and it's not about building up momentum or anything like that."

"What about going to therapy? What about getting antidepressants?"

"I'm not there yet, Kelsey. I'm just trying to keep my head above water. Will you let me do that?"

I force a smile. I'm not sure what to say.

"Listen, honey, I want you to go to the sleepover tomorrow. Get out of the house. Do something fun with your friends."

I bite my tongue.

More than anything I want to tell her that I'm going to a concert and I want her to stop me. I want her to ground me so that we can stay home and watch movies and do nothing. But I keep my mouth shut for my friends.

Besides, I'm not really sure if she would prevent me from going and that worries me, too. It's almost like she's become a completely different version of herself. She tells me that she's tired and that she has to leave now and I know that she's just going to go to her room and stare at the walls.

I hate being home.

I hate it more than anything because Dad is never here to deal with the consequences of what he has done. I can't make Mom leave him and I can't make her change. I wish more than anything that his girlfriend hadn't left him and that had actually spurred her to get a divorce and move on with her life. But maybe that would be even worse. I mean, if she got what she wanted, and she's this depressed, what would have happened if she didn't?

I grab my bike and take off and go to the beach because that's where they have dogs and I'm able to pet them freely. They're friendly and they love to run and play fetch.

A rambunctious Springer Spaniel barks at me until I throw the ball for her a number of times, and then we become best friends.

This isn't a great place to surf so I'm surprised when I see Liam walking down the shore of the Belmont Shore dog beach. Then I see his lab, and I know why he's here. I wave hello to him and he smiles at me ear to ear.

I've only met him a few times at school. He knows that I'm friends with Stephanie and we make small talk. The dog is a good distraction and I find out that his name is Tango. Something that his parents let him name him when he was a kid.

"What are you all doing this weekend?" he asks.

That's a veiled question about Stephanie's plans.

"I asked her if she wanted to go bowling with a few friends of mine. Maybe you girls can come."

"Yes, that sounds fun, but we actually have some work to do and I'm going to sleep over at a friend's house," I say, being vague on purpose.

In order to keep this lie a secret and protect Stephanie, we decided to not tell anyone about the concert. If it's particularly good, we will tell others afterward, but not before, so that our plans don't get thwarted.

"Oh, okay," Liam says, clearly disappointed.

"Stephanie's doing that, too?" he asks, double-checking.

"Yeah. She's going to Briana's house," I say and then realize that it doesn't quite make sense.

"But why are you not all together?"

"Clara's mom didn't want to have so many people over," I say, making up a lie on the spot and feeling bad about it.

Stephanie should at least tell him, I decide, but it's my secret to keep.

3

KELSEY

We are packed in like sardines and that's exactly the way we like it. Charlotte Pierce is wearing dark jeans, low cut, with a midriff-bearing tank. She has a nice body with just enough curves to pull something like that off. Her hair is down, blow-dried, and ironed as flat as possible to match the Avril Lavigne vibe. Southern California punk culture is very different from Seattle where the world of grunge still dominates the culture even though it has been almost ten years since the death of Kurt Cobain.

Sunshine Octopus is my favorite, however. They're opening for Avril and their songs, "Over Them All" and "Through the Sunshine" have been going on rotation on my CD player. Stephanie's clothes are nothing remarkable. She doesn't even attempt being cool and looks like her mom has dressed her. She did change out of her turtleneck into a t-shirt which I appreciate so that we don't look like we are accompanied by a chaperone. I still haven't told her what happened with Liam at the beach, and now I don't know if I can or should.

On Monday morning she'll probably find out, but I can wait until then, right? I don't want to ruin the concert. Or is it better to come forward now?

The intricacies of our relationship and what I owe to her in terms of girl code are confusing. I had friends back home but no romantic entanglements with their boyfriends.

We all meet up at a bus stop on Second Avenue and give each other warm hugs as we burst with excitement. We've told plenty of lies to our parents but somehow it is all justified in order to have everyone go and for the lies to be hard to check.

When I left this afternoon I left with a bag. It's a sleepover after all, and we're all going to stop at the motel first to drop off our things and finish getting ready.

Briana, of course, wants to touch up her eyeshadow. It's never dark enough, and she's even talking about trying on fake lashes.

"Like something that Marilyn Monroe wore in the '60s?" Charlotte asks in shock.

"Yes, it's actually pretty common in Hollywood. I mean, it makes your eyes really pop. You'll see. In the years to come, everyone will be wearing them."

"I don't believe it," Charlotte says as Briana opens her compact and tweezes her thin eyebrows to an even slimmer point.

"Can you believe how thick eyebrows were in the early '90s? I mean, I see those pictures of the models and it's just shocking."

"Well, it's fashion," Clara says. "It may come back. Plus it's not obligatory of you to follow every single thing that the magazines say."

"But then how will I know if I'm dressing properly?" Briana asks without a tinge of irony or sarcasm.

The bus ride is uneventful and we get there quickly. It's a Motel 6 with very few amenities. Two double beds. At least it's clean but the people outside are less than ideal. The guy leaning on the side of the building looks like he's willing to sell us some drugs and Briana is probably willing to take him up on the offer.

"Look, I'm sure there'll be plenty at the venue. We probably won't even have to pay for whatever weed we get," I say.

The financial argument brings her over to my side and I hope that she forgets all about it, or at least can bum a cigarette from one of the other concertgoers. The last thing I want to do is to get arrested or caught with marijuana on me, and I know that Charlotte, given the fact that her dad is an FBI agent, is also less than pleased by that possibility.

She and I are probably the closest of the group even though she and Clara seem to have a lot in common as well. She's friendly and outgoing, and I know the fact that she doesn't have a mom looms large even though she rarely talks about it.

Her dad leaves her alone a lot, which she says is a good thing, but she's been cooking for herself since she was eight, and it must get lonely to spend all that time alone.

Once we get into our seats and the show starts, my concerns, worries, and thoughts about my friends all vanish. I lose myself in the music the way that I have always done. Outside of fashion, it's my number one passion. I listen to music constantly while I'm studying, doing problem sets. Mom and Dad think I'm kidding, that I can't possibly be productive while having music in rotation blasting out of my room, but they're wrong about that.

In the silence is when I can't think. That's when my thoughts start to encroach and I daydream and think about other things and I can't focus. Recent obsession, my parents' marriage. How banal and boring is that?

When Avril Lavigne comes on and begins to sing, I lose myself in the energy of the space around me. The five of us jump up and down and laugh and scream out the words. If it's true what the Buddhists say about being one and present in a moment, it's true for me here, right now, just like everyone else in this arena.

Nothing else matters except for this.

Two hours is not nearly enough but after the last songs are sung and she comes back for an encore, it's time to leave.

Charlotte drinks too much. Everyone starts to have stomach pains because while we weren't able to find any weed, we did sneak in some alcohol and we all indulged. I didn't drink as much as some of the others, so I'm not retching in the bathroom.

I forget my scarf at my seat and leave the girls in the bathroom to throw up the rest of their dinners.

God, I hope they feel better by the time we get to the motel, I say to myself, hoping that the night doesn't conclude with them just all falling asleep and me staying up doing nothing.

I scramble past the crowds lingering in their seats, find my scarf and head back but I get lost somehow, take a wrong turn and end up outside. Afterward, no matter how much I argue with the security guards, they won't let me back in.

"If your friends are coming out, they'll be out shortly. Don't you have a phone?"

"No," I say.

Some people have a few of those Nokia phones but I don't and so they tell me to just wait out front of the main gate and they're sure that I'll run into them. I don't know how to contact them about me not being inside anymore and I hope that they just wander out eventually, but two hours later they're still nowhere to be found.

I wonder if they came out from another gate and decided to go to the motel. We hadn't explicitly decided to meet up there but that's the only other place I can imagine them going to, especially if they're sick and not in the mood to look and search for me.

I wait another forty-five minutes checking the gates, meandering around, and knowing full well that me leaving the front main entrance means that there's a likelihood that they had wandered out at the precise moment that I was checking one of the side gates.

The frustration and the boredom get the best of me. My throat is parched and I'm hungry so I decide to make the walk back to the motel to wait for them in the place that they absolutely have to go to tonight.

I make it a little bit down the street when a guy a few years older than me in a red convertible pulls up. He's got long, shaggy hair and he asks if I need a ride.

"No, I'm good," I say.

"Are you going far?" he asks, slowing down to a crawl.

There's nothing remotely threatening about him. He's easy on the eyes, has a sweet demeanor, but I know better.

"Nope."

"Okay," he says. "Hey, do you go to Adams?"

"Yes." I nod.

"Cool, my brother goes there, too. Eighth grade?"

I nod again.

"Excited for high school? I'm in 11th," he says.

He looks a bit younger but I'll take it. "Nice car."

"Yes, I just got my license. Parents got divorced so they're both trying to outdo each other with gifts. I'm not going to stop them."

"Wow, so what did your mom get you?" I ask. "A red convertible is pretty hard to beat."

"A trip to Hawaii with a few friends of mine. She chaperoned but she usually lets us do our own thing so we can surf the North Shore and get into trouble."

"Wow, to have parents like yours," I joke.

"To be honest, the divorce was the best thing that ever happened."

As I continue to walk down the street, he rolls along in his car and we talk back and forth.

"I wish my parents would get divorced," I tell him. "I'm tired of all the bickering and their cold war."

"Yeah, I know what you mean. That's how my brother and I were, but now my dad moved to the beach and has a fiancée. They want to have kids right away."

"Wow, maybe no more convertibles for you."

"He sells cars for a living so this is a tax write-off if anything," he jokes. "And if I can get into USC, it's all paid for."

"Lucky you," I say. It sounds like he's showing off but it feels like he's just talking nonchalantly to anyone who could hear.

We get to a red light and a car gets behind him.

"You're sure you don't want that ride? I won't be able to drive three miles an hour the whole way over."

"Are you sure it's not a problem?" I ask.

"Yes, of course. It's what, a mile from here?"

"Yes. About that, I think," I say. "I'm a little confused now as to where it is."

"Well, get in. We'll find it. What's it called?" he asks.

I climb in and he gives me a big wide smile. He's older with a nice car. He's also precisely the kind of guy that my dad would hate and that's just the cherry on top.

"How could I have ever gotten so lucky," I say to myself. The light turns green and we drive into the darkness.

4

CHARLOTTE

With a number of days off ahead of us, Dylan and I sleep in and don't leave for Vegas until 10:00 a.m. the following morning. This is the second time he's slept over at my house and I've yet to be to his. It already feels like we've known each other a long time and have been together forever. Our first date was a three-hour trip there and a three-hour trip back to the California state line. An overnight trip to Vegas for a long weekend doesn't seem like a stretch.

He's an easy guy to be with, well read and thoughtful. With some of the other men in this line of work, law enforcement seems to be the only thing they know anything about. That's all they've ever done or ever been interested in. Dylan, not so much. He worked as a detective in San Francisco, a cop before that, but he also has a degree in classics, loves Roman history, and reads plenty of fantasy and sci-fi.

The drive through the desert is breathtaking, blue skies, creosote bushes, Joshua trees, and giant rock formations.

We get out a few times to take pictures on the scramble of boulders to stretch our legs. There's no Wi-Fi here, it's spotty at best, but we talk nonstop about things we like, don't like, our passions, hopes, and dreams. It's like we can't get enough of each other. We can't talk enough, get a feel for what each other thinks and how we are in the world. We grew up with different families, different ways of being in the world, and yet we have so much in common.

I know nothing about ancient history and he promises to take me to Italy and Rome, a place he has been to once but loves so much that he seems to want to move there.

"You'll just love all the museums," he says. "There's so much art, beauty. It's breathtaking, and there are ruins all around the city and there's the Colosseum."

"You mean that death pit where people fought and lost their lives?"

"Yes, but it was so long ago that there's a kind of romance to it, don't you think?" He smiles ironically.

He's well aware of the fact that the Roman emperors were largely murderers and dictators, but that doesn't stop him from finding them utterly fascinating or him transferring that knowledge onto me.

"I've never been to Italy," I say. "Just been to London once, which I loved, and would love to go again."

"Oh my god, we have to do a whole European tour," he says. "London, Paris, Rome, Switzerland, or maybe we can just go there for half a year and travel around. Scandinavia is supposed to be amazing."

"I've read a lot of thrillers set there and, yes, Oslo and Iceland are definitely on my list," I say, "and so is Tuscany, of course. What writer or want-to-be writer doesn't see the allure of Tuscany?"

"What about Greece?" he asks. "The islands, the sailing? I'm going to build a boat in my garage. Did I tell you about that?"

"No. Wait, what?"

"Well, it's kind of a pipe dream, more of a canoe now, but yes. Besides going to Europe, my other big life dream is to get a sailboat and sail around the Caribbean."

"Wow, you're such a romantic," I say, "and you call yourself a detective."

"Well, not anymore. Now I'm a fireman."

"Hopefully, with the fireman's pension," I say jokingly. "Because you sure do have big dreams."

"Hey, I'm just going to wait for you to write a few novels, get really famous, and you can support me. How about that?"

"Hmm, if I could support you with my writing, then I'd say, sure, why not? because that's not really working."

"You don't think so?" he asks.

"No, not at all."

"You can write your music and compose. You can write and compose your symphonies on the piano, right?" I joke, bringing up another one of his hobbies.

"I honestly have no idea how you have time for work," I add. "Or relaxation. Your days seem to be filled with all of these things you do."

"Yes, that's true." He tilts his head.

"But you've got to have interests, right?"

"I'm not really into sports, except for basketball, so when I'm not working, I like to do other things."

"I can see that," I say. "I think that's what I like most about you. You have so many interests, passions. It's not as common as you think."

"No?" he asks.

"Not at all. I can't remember the last time I talked about Caesar Augustus at 10:00 a.m. in the morning on a drive to Vegas."

"Have you made a lot of drives to Vegas with guys you've been sleeping with?" He looks at me with a coy smile.

"You know what I mean." I laugh. "The things that we have talked about and we *are* talking about. That's not common. I mean, you've been on dates."

"Yeah, you're right. I've brought all of that up before and the girl usually falls asleep and stops responding to my texts. I guess I've been going about it all wrong."

I smile.

"But my wife and I talked about that stuff before," he adds.

"Oh, yes, of course."

I remember that he hasn't been single as long as I have. He hasn't been dating, subjecting himself to the dregs of society, all the people that haven't been taken or have been rejected by the time you're in your early 30s.

He told me a while ago that his wife died in a car accident. I can still see that it's painful for him to talk about.

"You know you can talk about her anytime you want to," I say. "I'd love to know more, but I don't want to pressure you if you're not ready."

"Thanks. I appreciate that. There's nothing really to say. We were together for years. She was the other person who tolerated my conversations about the Colosseum and Roman emperors and Caesar."

"Mmm, maybe I'm a keeper then." I smile.

"I think so." Dylan nods, reaching over and giving my hand a squeeze.

———

WE GET to the Vegas strip in early afternoon and pull up to the valet.

"You want to walk around here and grab dinner?" I ask. "It's really beautiful."

"No, this is where we're staying. Grab your things."

"You did not book the Bellagio," I say, looking at him. It's a five-star hotel that I've only walked through to take pictures of their elaborate flower-themed displays, but never actually stayed in.

"I had a lot of points on my card. I haven't gone anywhere for a while."

"Come on, be serious."

"Listen, I want to make this trip special. We can stay here. I work crazy overtime, and so do you, but this is all my treat."

I protest a little more, but eventually give in. After dropping off our bags, we return downstairs to walk through the lobby. Inspired by the sights, sounds, and scents of the season, the 14,000 square foot Botanical garden is redesigned every three months. This time it features fanciful hot air balloons, hummingbirds, and thousands of flowers that are an explosion of purple, yellows, blues, and pinks. The focal point of each garden is a huge balloon that makes it feel like you're walking through lavender woods and floating on clouds. There are woodland creatures and big flowers, all made out of living matter. There are giant cats and rabbits peeking out from behind bushes. Their ears are made from daffodils and daisies.

"I don't even know how they go about making these things," I say, looking closely at one of the ears, resisting the temptation to touch it. Instead, I take a picture. "They do this for different seasons and holidays. It's really beautiful. One of my favorite spots to walk through, but I have to be honest. I've never stayed the night."

"First time, huh?" Dylan asks.

"Yes, me, too." I smile.

Vegas is a common destination for west coasters and I've been here a few times. We have a couple of shows planned, but the first isn't until tomorrow night.

After we have dinner at Spago, we wander around the casino playing Black Jack and poker. I lose a hundred and win one-twenty. Since I'm ahead, I decide to quit and watch as Dylan loses $300, wins $100, and starts down another losing streak.

"You have to stop," I say. "I want to have money for dinner tomorrow and I don't want this trip to cost thousands of dollars."

He agrees with a laugh.

"Let's try our luck tomorrow?" I ask him and he smiles.

"Sure."

Late at night, we head back to our room and he kisses me in the elevator and I kiss him back. We're comfortable with each other now, somewhat familiar with each other's movements. There aren't many, but it's only our third night together and I'm excited to explore each other's bodies.

There's a big clawfoot tub in the marble bathroom, which he fills up and throws a bath bomb into. The room explodes with the scent of lavender. Dylan gives me an oil massage on the bed and leads me to the tub. I sit down with my back to him, playing with soap bubbles and feeling his body against mine.

"I like this," he says, nibbling on my earlobe, running his tongue along my neck.

I turn my face toward him and we kiss, our mouths soft, firm, and loving all at the same time. I lose myself in his hands, his flat stomach, and washboard abs.

But somewhere in the back of my mind, I can't help but remember that the reason we're here in Vegas is Kelsey, the girl who went missing all those years ago. The reason we're here is because of the secret that we all kept and the lies that we have told.

I'm going to see her after twenty years to try to make amends.

Will she be able to forgive me?

Will she recognize me? Will she remember me?

And if it is her, then why didn't her DNA match the real Kelsey Hall?

5

CHARLOTTE

The first time we approach Kelsey's house, she isn't home and I leave her house somewhat relieved. I want to see her but I don't. My mind goes in circles. For now, the inevitable has been postponed, and I'll take that as a win.

The wave of relief catches me by surprise. It's like when you have a test to take that you are poorly prepared for. You show up to school and the teacher's absent or they forgot the test papers at home. It's a little bit of a reprieve. You think you're going to study more tonight and prepare better, but in reality, you know that you probably won't.

I jump back into the car and drive out into the desert. I look at the GPS, narrow it down to where the developments end, and then pull out onto the side of the road and walk away. Dylan follows me.

"What are you doing?"

"Going for a hike," I say.

We walk for a good half mile, deeper and deeper into the creosote bushes, closer to the red rocks out in the distance. The ground is uneven, full of shrubs and rocks; a few lizards go back and forth across the path, There's no trail here at first, but I stumble upon one and follow it going nowhere in particular.

Dylan seems to have a sixth sense about when to speak and when not to.

He doesn't press. He doesn't push.

He just lets me go, giving me time to think.

"You want to see her, right?" he asks after a while when I slow down a little bit. My steps aren't as frantic and I start to enjoy the natural world around me.

"Of course I do. That's why I came here. I was just happy that she wasn't there. It's hard to explain."

"I know exactly how you feel. All the buildup happened, and then nothing and the wave of relief, right?"

I nod. "I've had that when I've had to interview some suspects, the dangerous kind. Mostly the ones you don't really want to talk to in a dark alley."

"But this is Kelsey."

"Yes, but it may not be her. We think it's her but it may not be," I say. "I don't know if you know this about me, but I'm not one for confrontation. This job, the interrogation, is something that I had to learn. I'm not innately good at it like some people. I don't like catching people in lies. I don't like to challenge them. I don't like to lie myself to try to get them to admit to something."

"Then maybe being a detective isn't the best option you." He smiles, tilting his head in that cocky way. His hands are in the pockets of his jeans that make his butt look, oh, so good.

"Yes, it's a funny, odd life choice, isn't it?" I smile. "I like other things about it and I thought I could grow into it, but this is Kelsey. This is my friend from 8th grade. This is my past and all the lies that we've told and all the secrets that we've kept. It's just a little overwhelming."

I lean over resting my hands on my knees and then drop down completely, burying my head in my legs. This is a yoga pose. It's supposed to be relaxing.

Clearing the tension from the back of your spine. It does until I get up again, broaden my shoulders, and realize just how much I have been holding there and how hunched over I've been during this whole hike.

In the distance, I see a woman with a Labrador heading toward us. She's taking some photos, and when she gets closer, I can see there's a little baby strapped to her stomach in a carrier. She gives us a pearly white smile and walks by as her yellow lab wags her tail with excitement.

"I can't remember the last time my life was normal," I say to Dylan. "Like that woman there. She has a baby, husband probably, walking her dog, talking about how well the baby's sleeping, all that stuff. She probably has mom friends where they talk about nothing in particular. To tell you the truth, I would love that."

"You won't miss this life looking for murderers?"

"No."

"Dealing with missing persons, dead kids?"

"Of course, I love it when it all turns out okay. Somebody's found like with Madison Dillard, but that's not always the case, as you know."

I thought that coming to Mesquite County would slow my life down, make it a little bit more manageable, but I realize that small rural and suburban communities have just as many problems as urban ones and the workload can be just as grueling.

"Well, you can do something else," Dylan offers.

"The problem is that I can't. I have no skills; have no experience in anything else. The only thing I can imagine doing is possibly writing for a living but is that even possible or is that just some dream? That's a reality for a few select people out there and no one else."

"I guess you'll never know until you finish your book." Dylan smiles and gives me a reassuring hug. "Look, I know you're nervous about meeting Kelsey, but you'll never know if it's her for sure, until you do. Why not get it out of the way? Just go for it."

"You mean show up at her house again or call her?"

"She might not be there because she's at work or something like that but I feel this thing weighing on you. You won't be able to enjoy these days off if you don't just pull the Band-Aid off."

"You're one of those people that jumps into a cold body of water right away, aren't you?" I ask.

"Of course, don't you?"

"No." I smile. "I inch my way in waiting for all my extremities to go numb."

"Wow. If that's not a metaphor for how different we are, I don't know what is."

I give him a wink, pulling out my phone. "I'm going to give her a call."

"Okay."

Luckily I have enough reception and I dial the number. On the third ring, just as I'm about to leave a message, a female voice answers.

"My name is Charlotte Pierce and I'd love to have a chance to chat with you about some of the things you shared with Jonathan Chabon."

"Charlotte?" the woman on the other end asks. "I don't recognize your voice but the hesitation is familiar; the enunciation is as well. It's really you, isn't it?"

"Kelsey, can you possibly meet?" I ask, trying to hold back a wave of emotion that rushes over me.

"Yes. I'm just out running errands, but I'll be back at my house at like one o'clock. Can you do that?"

"Yes."

She hangs up before I can say bye. I look at Dylan who gives me a reassuring smile.

"That was her," I whisper.

"Are you sure?"

"Yes." I nod.

6

CHARLOTTE

The second time we arrive at her house, Kelsey opens the door before I even bring my hand up to knock. She was waiting, looking out the window. The little yapper dog continues to bark, but she's all noise, no bite. I even kneel down to the floor to give her a little hug.

Kelsey and I don't know how to be with one another. When I rise back up to my feet, we shake hands and I introduce Dylan as a friend and a retired detective from San Francisco to give him a little bit more credence and a reason to be here.

She's a few inches taller than I am in wedges. Her toenails are perfectly manicured and painted pastel green. It's warm outside and she's wearing a bright yellow floral summer dress, lightweight and casual. It accentuates her figure, her tan skin, and her blown-out long hair.

I remember a girl who used to wear only black or mostly black to look sophisticated. Now I see someone who could be walking out of the Bravo reality show, *Real Housewives of Las Vegas*. My black slacks and white dress shirt that's a little drenched in sweat and limp at the collar looks less than professional and less than attractive.

Despite the changes in her appearance and her demeanor, she's undoubtedly Kelsey Hall, my friend, and the person that I owe an apology to.

Her kitchen is all white marble countertops with an island with a few green cactus plants thrown in for color. It looks like it's straight out of a magazine. I can see that her interest in fashion, things like that have not diminished with age. If anything, she can pay for them now.

We sit around her round marble table on the gray mid-century modern chairs with brushed gold legs. She offers us coffee and tea and pours herself a glass of orange juice. Dylan opts for the same.

"I can't believe it's you," she says, shaking her head, "and you're a cop?"

"Yes, detective, Mesquite County Sheriff's Department."

"Wow. That's impressive."

"She used to work for the LAPD," Dylan pipes in to try to talk up my credentials.

"But then I moved out to the desert," I say.

"Hey, I get it. I'm not going back to Seattle or Long Beach anytime soon. I love it out here in Vegas. Something about the blue sky and the complete lack of rain just kind of puts you in a happy mood every day, doesn't it? No need to worry about the weather bringing you down. I remember I used to love the rain, talked about how much the fog at the beach reminded you of Seattle. That was another life, wasn't it?"

I'm not sure how to broach what had happened.

Kelsey doesn't seem to want to talk about it and I give her space. She asks me about my life, and I fill her in using big brush strokes.

When she asks about my dad who she knew back then, I tell her that he's now the Deputy Director of the Federal Bureau of Investigation, not just a special agent.

"That's pretty impressive," she mumbles.

I wonder how much influence she thinks that all these people who are involved in law enforcement had on her missing person's search.

"What about you?" I ask. "Tell me about you. How long have you been living in Vegas?"

"A number of years. My husband's a criminal attorney. We met because he represented me in a case."

"What do you mean?" I ask.

"I wasn't arrested for anything, but I reached out to him to help me deal with the police and everything that has happened. He used to live in California, but then we decided to move to Vegas."

She's dancing around the story about what happened in the past, touching on it lightly but not really elaborating.

"We have children now. They're in school. I'm just your normal stay-at-home wife, participate a lot with the PTA, raise money for their school, doing bake sales and I love it."

"You do?"

"Yes. It's everything that I never wanted when I was a kid and then desperately wanted when…I was gone."

"I can only imagine," I whisper.

"Are you going to be in town for a few days?" she asks.

I nod.

"Good."

"Can I ask you something?" I ask. "Your family, they're aware of what happened?"

"My children are too young still. They know something bad happened and that's why they don't have grandparents on mommy's side, but we haven't gone into all the details. I'm working with a psychologist to slowly unfold the pieces of the onion and tell them about how everything that happened and that kind of thing. My husband, yes, he knows everything and how much the cops messed up."

There it is. There's my opening.

"I want to apologize," I say. "I don't want to make excuses or say that I was young and stupid, even though both of those things are true. The cops should have pushed us harder on our story. They should have interviewed our parents or made any effort to go deeper into what we had said. That's a basic interrogation protocol. We would have caved, but none of that changes what happened to you and I'm sorry. I'm sorry that I lied to the cops. I'm sorry that we all did about your disappearance."

She nods.

"What did you tell them exactly?" Kelsey asks slowly.

Even if she didn't know this part of the story, she deserves to, and I don't care anymore.

If she thinks that it's right for her to sue me, then so be it. I want all of this to come out. I want people to know the truth.

"When you went to look for your scarf, we waited for you, but you didn't come back. I went to look for you and couldn't find you. We went to the motel room hoping that you would be there, and you weren't. The next morning, we didn't report it. When the cops came looking for you because your parents called them when you didn't come home, we told them the story that we all came up with earlier about sleeping over at each other's houses and all of that crap. They took it at face value."

Kelsey shakes her head.

"They interviewed me once," I continue. "They assumed that you went missing sometime that evening and maybe even ran away by yourself because of some issues you had with your parents. No one came knocking on my door. No one asked for the truth, but for what it's worth, I know that we were wrong. If we had just gone to the security guards and told them about your being there, your disappearance, some report would have been filed. The police at the arena would have been notified and maybe--"

"They wouldn't have found me," Kelsey says. "I got into this guy's car. It was a red convertible. He was friendly and outgoing and told me that his brother went to our school. I trusted him. He told me he would give me a ride to the motel, but then drugged me with something at a stoplight. I remember him and I don't remember anything past that. He kidnapped me or was working with someone who then trafficked me."

"What happened?" I ask.

"The next months and years are a blur, a lot of drugs, prostitution, moving around from place to place. There were other girls there. I didn't know where I was. There were just motel rooms, seedy apartments, that kind of thing. Sometimes they would have windows, sometimes they wouldn't. Some days I didn't even know whether it was day or night, fall, spring, summer, or winter. The johns would come and we'd have to do what they said. I became addicted to a whole concoction of drugs, and after a while, they made me start paying for them myself out of the measly pay that I got. It's actually quite banal and boring and happens all the time."

"I'm so sorry, Kelsey," I say.

"I use another name now, but you can still call me Kelsey."

"I understand. But what about Jonathan's article?"

"I read some stuff he wrote and there was a story that matched mine. I just reached out to him because it sounded like something that happened to me. I remembered a little bit about that night, but it took me a while to even recollect that my name was Kelsey. That's how shock and drugs, and everything that I've been through. His story lined up."

She pauses for a moment and takes a deep breath.

"So, what happened then?" I prod her.

"He reached out to my parents. They wanted a DNA confirmation. I guess I don't fault them because they got scammed by somebody else. You won't believe how many scammers try to take advantage of people's grief and get them to pay some ransom. I figured my DNA would be, of course, a match, but then it wasn't, and I just started having doubts about everything. Maybe I wasn't Kelsey Hall. I don't know, maybe I made up the whole story. Maybe I wanted to believe that I was her because there was some black and white proof of me actually existing on paper in this article. But now you're here, and you're Charlotte. I remember you, and I remember your father. I remember the fun that we had."

"I'm so sorry, Kelsey," I say. "I'm sorry, I didn't mean to say that name."

"No, actually, come to think of it, it's okay. You know me as Kelsey, maybe it's okay that you call me that."

I reach across the table and pull her close to me. At first, she resists, but then she buries her head in my shoulder and begins to cry.

"You are *her*," I whisper. "I know it for sure. I don't care what the DNA says."

"But why doesn't it match?" She pulls away from me, tears streaming down her face. Her mascara doesn't leak at all, probably waterproof, but her face is streaked from the trails that her tears leave in her foundation.

"I'm so sorry about everything, but I knew immediately that it was you. Have you tried to reach out to your parents and maybe just go over there to their house and talk to them? If I recognized you, then they would, too, I'm sure."

"No, I can't," Kelsey says, shaking her head. "I'd rather just leave it where it is. If they don't want to see me, if they gave up on me, then that's fine."

"They're still together," I say. "I remember they were having all those issues, but they went back to Seattle after your disappearance and they've been together ever since. I don't know whether it's happily or not though."

Kelsey pulls away from me.

"We were arguing a lot right before the concert," she says. "I wanted my mom to leave. I wanted her to stand up for herself. I didn't want her to be treated like crap and put up with my dad's cheating. But she refused. I'm sure my disappearance was just the thing they needed to pull back together as one couple."

"You can't blame them."

"Yes, I can," she snaps. "I can blame them a lot. Maybe not for going missing initially and for all the lies that you all told. The people that took me, they were smart. I doubt that we were even in California that night despite your lie. I'm not trying to get you off the hook, but it was all very planned."

I nod.

"But as far as my parents are concerned," Kelsey continues. "All they had to do was get on Zoom with me, just to see. I didn't even have to go through the DNA test. They'd known, and I know they knew, and they just don't want to know. Maybe they don't want a broken daughter back. Who knows?"

"I'm really sorry about not being a better friend back then. I guess we'll never know what happened or what our lies could have prevented or changed, but I want to make you a promise. I'm going to figure out what happened to that DNA test and why it didn't match. I want to do that for you because well, I've fallen so short in everything else in our friendship."

Kelsey looks into my eyes wiping the last of her tears. She smiles a little out of the corner of her mouth.

"Yes, I'd like that. If you can help in any way, I'd appreciate it."

7

CHARLOTTE

I talk to Kelsey for a couple of hours, and then she says that she has to go to pick up her kids, but we should keep in touch. We make no firm plans about the rest of my visit here, but I know that I will talk to her on the phone again, maybe video chat, and definitely visit.

Driving back to the strip, I lose myself in my thoughts about everything that has happened. The lie about that night weighed on me for so many years that I suddenly feel incredibly light.

I share this with Dylan and he gives me a reassuring squeeze of the hand but doesn't say that it's okay. I appreciate that.

For years, I just dwelled on it, thought about her, where she was, and my contribution to her disappearance. It's probably one of the reasons why I decided to go into law enforcement. Even when I did, I just never thought that I was ready to pursue this case.

Little did I know that it was already solved and figured out. She was, luckily, found, saved, fine.

"How do you feel about it now?" Dylan asks.

"Conflicted. I'm so happy that it's her and she's doing so well, but those years were difficult. If I had stumbled upon her just ten years earlier, who knows what help I could have provided or anything else?"

"There're some people who come in and out of our lives," Dylan says. "They're these effervescent particles present but not present. I think you can be that for her now. You can be that touchstone so that she knows that in her past life, everything that she experienced wasn't just something she made up."

"Yes, she was struggling with that."

"She lost so many years but finding out the truth about the DNA will go a long way to making amends."

"You don't think that I should just go to Seattle and tell them that I actually met with her?" I ask.

"I don't know. Maybe. Why wouldn't it match? Was there a mistake at the lab? What else could have happened?"

"Yes." I nod. "You're right, I have to bring them some proof. They've been through a lot, too, despite their issues with her and all their problems. She's their daughter. Their only daughter. Their only child. It must be excruciating knowing that she disappeared never to be heard from again."

THE REST of the weekend is a blur, but a good blur.

We gamble. We win some; we lose some.

We eat a lot of food, spend way too much money in fancy restaurants sitting around, talking about nothing in particular, and just enjoying each other's company.

Kelsey comes up occasionally, but I try to leave her aside. This is my trip, my time off from work, and Dylan's, too. It's important to make space and time and to corner off your life for something to care about.

The last night we're here, we go see *The Beatle's LOVE* show. Then, afterward, we are walking past the club at the casino and he asks if I want to dance.

"I do."

I had two drinks and I feel light on my feet.

"I'm not a good dancer," I say.

"Good, that makes both of us."

Dylan grabs my hand, pulling me close to him. The energy in the room is thumping, bodies colliding; everyone in stilettos, short dresses, looking their best, their hottest.

Under these lights and this music, I lose myself in Dylan. He is a much better dancer than I am and spins me around effortlessly leading me in my movements.

He makes his way around my body knowing exactly which curves to glide against. There's not one awkward move. I grab onto his butt and give it a squeeze. He turns me on as we grind against each other.

My theory is that the reason that women love to dance is that it's foreplay. You take a guy out on a test ride so to speak, see how he is with handling your body and whether he's worth taking to bed.

Dylan's an expert. He puts me to shame, but he's also a class act who never says a mean word about my lack of good moves.

"How did you learn how to dance like this?" I ask, running out of breath.

"My mom taught dance for little kids. I didn't really like it much at first, but she said that I had to learn some moves. It would be my superpower."

"Well, it kind of is. It's not that many men who can dance like you, and, man, I can't pull away."

"Don't."

He pulls me close, my body against the hardness of his. I let my fingers run down his chest feeling every indentation of his six-pack. He smiles, grabs my hand, and twirls me around, pulling me close again.

After an hour of dancing, I realize that I shouldn't fight it. I shouldn't do my own moves. I should just let him fling my body around and follow along mirroring his moves. That's when we start to move as one together.

"Glad my mom taught me how to dance," he says.

"Me, too," I whisper and kiss him.

All the noise, the crowd, the thumping music, it's almost like it's not here, and it's just the two of us alone dancing in each other's arms.

Our mouths collide, find each other, and the world fades away.

8

CHARLOTTE

After the weekend in Vegas, it's a slog to get back to work. I'm praying for a slow day with some time to ease into things but Will Torch, my sometimes partner, pulls me aside right away. He looks frantic, out of sorts, like he hasn't slept all night.

"I've got to talk to you," he says.

I raise my hand up. "No, not before I have some coffee. I had a nice weekend and I want to hold on to that memory for as long as possible."

"Another missing kid," he says. "We've got to go interview his parents, but you have some coffee. Take your time. Not like the bad guy isn't going to get away in the meantime."

I roll my eyes. He's right, of course. I pour the coffee, splashing it a little bit over the to-go cup, and head out to his vehicle. He's driving.

"You look like crap," I say.

"Thanks?" he answers with a question mark.

"Rough weekend?" I ask. He nods.

"Good rough or bad rough?"

"Good." He smiles.

"Things with Erin are fine?"

"Yes, she's great. It's like all that time that we were apart never passed. She wants to see me all the time. Can't get enough."

"Wow. What kind of drugs do you have her under?" I joke.

He rolls his eyes at me.

"You know, there are people out there that enjoy spending time with me. I know that's hard for you to believe."

"Yes, it is, but I guess anything is possible."

On the drive over, he fills me in about his weekend at the beach, not glossing over the precise number of times that they were intimate.

"You know we're friends, right? But you realize that I'm not your bro. Just thinking maybe you want to keep some things to yourself."

"I thought we had a real friendship," he says. "I mean, I thought we could tell each other anything."

"Yes, we can. Whether we should, that's a whole other thing."

"What about the lieutenant?" I ask. "Any news on that?"

This turns the conversation to a more serious tone.

At one point, Lieutenant Soderman ran into Will and Erin together at the movies and saw them making out, a clear violation of all police ethics since Erin was the primary suspect in the murder of her ex-husband and his wife.

Will and Erin knew each other from childhood and reconnected during the case. While the real murderer was found to be someone else, it was still a breach of protocol to pursue a relationship with her, in whatever capacity.

"If the lieutenant knows anything," Will says. "He's not talking. I mean, he hasn't brought it up once and now I wonder if it even happened at all."

"If you saw him and he saw you, it did," I assure him.

"I guess, but why didn't he bring it up yet? Why am I still on this case? Why was I on the last case with you?"

"Shortage of good detectives?" I suggest. "But, to be more honest, it's probably because he doesn't want to stir the pot. Maybe it's easier to pretend that he didn't see you and not open an internal affairs investigation on you. Who knows? Count your blessings and don't push the envelope."

"I want to ask her to marry me," Will says as we pull into a dusty neighborhood on the outskirts of town.

This is where development hasn't reached yet. The road is unpaved, complete western desert, just ten minutes outside of Palm Valley in the great expanse that is Mesquite County.

"You can't be serious." I look at him. "You and Erin have to keep all of this on the down low."

"Yes, I know, but for how long? The case is over. It wasn't her. She had nothing to do with it. Can I *never* date her? Never be with her?"

"I don't know, but the minute you show up with her as your fiancée or even girlfriend, there're going to be questions. When did your relationship start exactly? How long has it been going on?"

"What if we just lie about that part? What if we lie and say that we just ran into each other long after the case was closed and got together?"

"The trial is still going on," I remind him. "This case isn't closed and you know it. We know it's not her, but you're going to have to go on the stand and testify. You know that that defense attorney is going to use everything in his power against you; *this* included."

He nods and swallows hard.

"Then we have a problem," he says. "Erin's pregnant. It just happened. We didn't think that she could *get* pregnant and…"

I shake my head.

"It's happy news, Charlotte. Don't look at me like that. I love her. I'm glad she's in my life. I've realized that she is probably the only person I've ever loved and there's nothing wrong with that."

"Not normally, but you're a cop in a county where everyone thought she had committed a brutal double murder if not a triple murder because her ex-husband's new wife was pregnant. If you remember."

"Yes, I do remember," Will says, "more than anyone else, but this has to end sometime, right? At some point we can be together."

"At some point, yes. Now? No."

WE TURN onto a dirt road and drive for a little while. Out in the distance, I see a small house. It looks like a homesteader cabin that was built in the 1950s back when everything around here was just the wild west and not much else.

"I've never been out here," I admit. "Actually, I had no idea there were still houses like this around."

"Yes, a few. A bunch of developers are paying these people to move so they can build a big resort. An HOA community, but really upscale. Look at those views of the mountains from here, they're all covered in snow in the winter. The palm trees would flourish. It's just so beautiful."

At high noon, it is well over a hundred and the shadows are short. There are a few old palm trees circling the property, creating a privacy fence. Inside, we see a small house, maybe a thousand square feet. It's in a Spanish Revival-style, reminiscent of old California.

Right before I knock on the carved-wooden door, a couple walks out, clutching onto one another.

9

CHARLOTTE

Mr. Lansky is in his fifties or early sixties and Mrs. Lansky is probably in her mid-forties. This is my first time interviewing the Lanskys, but Will has already met them when they first made the initial report. Their six-year-old son had gone missing, riding his bike around the property. They have some cameras set up, but caught nothing on them of importance.

They welcome us into their Spanish-style home, the walls of which are adorned with Southwestern décor. There's a shoe rack to the side and both Lanskys are barefoot. I ask if we should remove our shoes, and she says, "No," in that way where you know that you probably should. I don't like to remove my shoes while I'm on the job especially since we'll have to walk the property soon and make notes.

We sit down on the rather uncomfortable leather sofa, which looks great, but is as hard as a rock. In their formal living room there's a painting of a large horse head. It's three dimensional and partly coming out of the painting. It's not exactly my style, but it somehow fits with the rest of the house. Mrs. Lansky has long, dark hair, and by long, I mean down to her waist. It's pulled up partly and held with a clip.

"Thank you for meeting with us again. As I said, this is my partner, Detective Charlotte Pierce, and she's going to be working the case with me. She was, unfortunately, unavailable last night."

They give me a slight nod. Mr. Lansky walks over to the bar on one end of the formal living room and makes himself a drink, offering us a whiskey.

"No, thank you. We're on the job," Will says. I wait for an offer of some water since my mouth is parched, but nothing comes and I don't press.

"Can you just repeat for us what you told me yesterday about how Ricky went missing?"

"I just don't know where he is," Mrs. Lansky says, starting to weep. "We looked everywhere. We had all of our friends and family walking the property and we saw nothing."

"Yes, the deputies were also here last night. We had an impromptu search, and since Mr. Lansky is an avid outdoorsman, he helped a lot with that," Will explains.

This all happened while I was on a trip to Vegas. Cases don't wait for you to start investigating. I'm just trying to catch up at this point.

"Can you just repeat the story so I can hear it firsthand?" I ask. "With any details that you remember, don't summarize."

When I touch her hand slightly, she recoils away from me.

"He went riding his bike around the property right here inside the gate like he always did. It was his favorite thing to do. He could do it for hours. We have almost two acres here, but the paved part is not that extensive," Mrs. Lansky begins. "We got him an off-road mountain bike, but it's quite rocky. He was getting a little annoyed, I guess. He kept asking for the last couple of days if he could leave the property and go down the big hill."

"The road down is paved all the way, but the road we drove up isn't?" I ask.

"We started paving the other road up here. It goes from the side of the property. It's not connected yet all the way to the main road."

"You're building your own?" I ask. They nod.

"The county was never going to do it. It was a cheaper and easier way to go from that direction. We started near our property and we're making progress, but it ends about a quarter of a mile down and it's just open desert again."

"You're going to connect that road to Oak Tree Hill?" I ask.

They nod.

"Yes, that's the plan."

"And that's where he was?" I ask.

"Yes, he kept asking to go outside the fence and we didn't want him to for a while but we figured, what could happen? It's just the desert out there. No one else. Why not?"

"How long was he out there?"

"I would check on him in half hour increments. It was getting hot and so this was going to be when he'd have to go in. Around four-thirty that afternoon, right before dinner time, I went out and he wasn't there. I thought he'd gone around somewhere else but I couldn't see him."

"You checked on him a few times and he was there?" I ask.

"Yes. He first went out around three. I checked on him at three thirty, four, and then four thirty."

"That's when he disappeared?"

She nods. "He just wasn't there."

"What about his bike?"

"No. Both were gone. My husband and I ran out there. We thought maybe he went out into the woods, out into the desert. We were trying to look for a trail from the bike but it wasn't there. It's like he just disappeared, and I have no idea what happened. That's when we called the police at six that evening after we looked and scoured that whole area."

"I just don't understand how he could have disappeared without a road in nearby," Mr. Lansky says. "I mean, if someone grabbed him they'd have to walk through the desert, and then where are the tracks for the bike? What could have happened?"

"I'm not sure. That's what we're here to find out. The search yesterday?" I turned to Will. "The deputies? How far did everyone get?"

"We searched probably three miles in a circle around the house focusing on that back road," Will says.

"We're going to do it again today right after this. That's when the volunteers are coming," Mrs. Lansky says.

"Okay. I'd like to be a part of that," I say. "We both would."

Luckily, I have my boots in the car. Something a little bit more appropriate for walking through the desert. I ask for more details about Ricky and they show me pictures. A smiling blond little boy with blue eyes and a tan face. In all the pictures, his knees are dirty, the kind of kid who clearly loves living outdoors.

The Lanskys show us out back where they have goats, chickens, and rabbits in a coop. It's a little hobby farm that Mrs. Lansky put together.

"We're getting Ricky a horse for his birthday, which is next month," she says. "This is going to be a surprise because he always wanted to learn how to ride one. He wants to be a cowboy."

Her voice cracks. I know what she's thinking.

"What if he's not back by then?" she whispers.

"We're going to do everything in our power to find him," I promise.

Mrs. Lansky nods, forces a smile, and I know that she's hoping against hope that I am right.

10

———

CHARLOTTE

It's eleven by the time we start the search. Deputies set up a grid approach and organize the volunteers into sections. With the desert terrain, we need as many people as possible to cover so many acres.

We move according to a grid. The terrain is sketched out and a certain number of people are assigned to an area. You move slowly, walking, looking around, keeping an eye out for anything that can be of use.

We're not just looking for a little boy, but his clothing, obviously his bike, shoes, and anything else that he might have been wearing. The Lanskys say that their son was wearing a little bracelet around his wrist. It's a Spiderman snap on bracelet that he got at a birthday party.

Their friends and family arrive bringing a lot of kids, all of his friends, which is non-ideal, for the search. We gather them outside under an awning in front of their garage. The inside of the house is declared a crime scene. The Lanskys were tentatively allowed to stay there because technically he went missing from outside the premises.

Will and I make our way toward where the pavement begins. In the distance, a group of volunteers and deputies have gathered for the search. I ask him about his impression about the Lanskys themselves. It's a well-known fact that when children go missing, most of the time it's a family member who's involved. It's an unfortunate result, but it does often make it easier to investigate than a stranger abduction, which are very hard to solve.

"I get the feeling that they are very concerned," Will says.

"They were completely distraught yesterday. Today it seems like they're more numb than anything."

I hate to say it, but I do believe them. They're worried about their kid. He spent a whole night out in the elements, which as you know, isn't good news.

"Yes. How long did the search go on last night?"

"Till five in the morning."

"Until daybreak, and nothing?"

Will shakes his head.

"Nope. We found nothing. Not the bracelet, not the shoes, not the bike, not the kid."

"Where could he have gone?" I ask as we make our way down a road that has been paved haphazardly.

It's not a city job with a big roller truck making the cement completely, perfectly straight. The ground underneath is probably not packed down all the way, but it did accomplish its job in that it doesn't pick up dust. A car that would go over here after a rainstorm wouldn't get muddy.

It's a smoother drive than over the desert for sure.

"The ground around here is like sand," I say, walking. In some places, there are rocks and gravel, Just hard, But right here, it's silt. I notice how my shoes practically disappear into the fine sand.

"If he dropped something," Will says, "and the wind came over the mountains, it could easily be covered up."

I think the same thing, pulling my foot out of the soft sand.

"It's going to make it even harder to find evidence," I say.

"We shouldn't have them digging yet."

"No," Will says. "Let's just do a traditional grid search. See what they find walking around without messing with possible evidence."

"What do you think we're doing here?"

A little bit of time passes and the sun starts to be on top of me. I'm carrying a water bottle and I suck up a few big gulps. Water bottles are pretty much a requirement here and mine is insulated. So the water is still ice cold and refreshing The only negative thing about it is that it's metal and rather heavy to carry.

"So what do you think?" I ask, taking a few slow steps, looking around carefully just like I have been for the last hour. "You think we're looking for a body at this point?"

"I don't know." Will shrugs. "I hate to say yes because it hasn't been long enough, but you know what they say. Kids missing for more than twelve hours, especially this young, there's no way he ran off. Someone probably took him and the bike."

"There were no marks from a car. There were no tracks from anything driving up that road. We would've seen those, unless he got out and covered his tracks somehow."

THE GRID SEARCH begins around eleven when most of the volunteers arrive to help. People are excited to be here, anxious to find out what happened and to help the Lanskys find their son. Will and I are in charge. We make our way to where they are gathered and give them a brief speech about what to do and what not to do. Mainly, don't touch anything and move very slowly looking for any evidence of anything, whatsoever.

We spread out and each volunteer covers a small distance of a grid. The ground has turned from soft and silty to rough and uneven. The white sand has all but disappeared. Right past where the pavement of the road ends, the harsher version of the desert has taken over. Big boulders, rocks, uneven ground. On the surface, this looks like a difficult place for a little boy and his bike to go missing.

Where would he go exactly? What would he do?

Something that I have yet to share with the Lanskys is that he might have been taken, he might have been hurt. I know that Will knows this as much as I do, but we're keeping hope alive, not wanting to go there exactly, not with all the darkness that it brings.

The volunteers, on the other hand, are eager, optimistic, and even excited. For most of them, this is their first real venture into police work and they're happy to be here.

It's easy to lose track of time when you do this work. You focus, but you can't focus forever so you let your mind wander. I start thinking about all the things that I could be doing right now besides this. My office back in my house needs a good bit of organizing. I recently bought a number of books that I want to put away and make all pretty and nice the way that shelves look on social media.

It's been a yearning of mine for some time to get out of this line of work. It's too depressing, too sad, but I am good at this job, and the department needs me. There are a few detectives that just don't measure up in their honesty, in their willingness to go the extra mile, and all the other features of a good investigator.

I saw that the department wouldn't exist without me. In fact, it would be worse, and we all know it. Will and I have talked about this a number of times when I mentioned leaving. I promised myself that for now, I'm going to stay, but that shouldn't stop me from figuring out what else I want to do with my life.

We make our way down the hill.

Someone yells, "There, I see something!"

The voice belongs to Maureen something. I can't remember her last name, but I met her as she's close friends with Mrs. Lansky. When Will and I rush over, she points to the half-buried bicycle lying there completely untouched, partly covered up with sand and rocks.

"This is it. This is his bike!" Mrs. Lansky yells as Will and I try to secure the scene.

We tell everyone to move over, stay clear, and put up posts to string caution tape and push people back. It works somewhat, but part of the reason why everyone has volunteered is to be part of the action.

The bike is partly covered with dirt like someone had thrown sand on it.

You can see a little bit of red on the bike's body, but the lights have been covered up along with the tires. In fact, I'm surprised that Maureen had spotted the bike at all because from a certain angle, you wouldn't be able to.

"What does this mean?" Mrs. Lansky turns to me, taking me by surprise.

"It means that he lost his bike," I say.

"But where is Ricky?" She presses.

"I'm really sorry, Mrs. Lansky. At this point, we have no idea, but we're going to continue the grid search in this direction. Let me just tape this off first. The deputies will stay behind and Detective Torch and I are going to go up ahead just in case."

The Lanskys try to protest, but the deputies wrangle them and the volunteers as Will and I head up the rocky hill.

"Where are you going?" Will asks, trying to catch up with me.

"I just want to get to the ridge. I think that will give us a good vantage point."

We do a cursory search, not detailed like the volunteers and like I would if we were walking slowly or looking for something big. I don't want to say "the body", but something visible.

"If the bike is here, there's a strong possibility that--" Then my mouth drops open.

Just over the ridge, we see Ricky's lifeless body, covered in dirt and dust.

Legs splayed out and arms, too.

His eyes are closed, and he's lying under the bright blue sky.

"There he is," I whisper and Will sees him, too.

"I'm going to tell them to hang back."

"Uh-huh," I say, taking a few steps closer and crouching down. I make sure that he is, in fact, deceased, but I don't touch him.

His lips are blue. Eyelids closed.

His chest isn't moving up and down with breath.

I don't want to touch him quite yet because I want CSI to collect the evidence, if any, but from the looks of it, something has happened. He's got bruises and contusions all over his face and his arms from what's visible underneath his clothes. The shirt is partly shredded as well.

Will returns and I hear the Lanskys' wails out in the distance, echoing around the hills.

"I told them, but the deputies are keeping them back for now."

"Thanks," I say.

"What do you think happened?" Will asks.

I shrug.

We examine the body.

"All those cuts and scratches could be a mountain lion," Will says.

I nod. "That's a very real possibility."

"So, what could have happened?" Will asks, thinking out loud. "He rode his bike, tripped, went over his bike, left it for some reason, and went over the ridge."

"He might have gotten off if he saw a mountain lion," I suggest. "Went over the ridge, maybe twisted his ankle, broke his leg. We won't know until the autopsy comes back."

"Couldn't move. Doesn't look like a mountain lion attack though," he says.

"Yes. I mean, there are scratches and there are plenty of those, but it doesn't feel like an animal attack."

"What does this mean?" Will asks.

"I'm really not sure. Do you see any harm or foul play from the outside?" I ask. "I mean, I don't see anything around his head or his back."

"What about all those rocks?" Will asks. "How did they get on top of him?"

"If the mountain lion dragged him, that might be a possibility. We have to check the weather to see how windy it was, but there still seems to be too much dirt on top of him."

"You think someone tried to bury him?" Will asks.

"We won't know anything until the evidence comes back," I say. "We just have to go and talk to the

Lanskys now. The CSI team has to come in, secure this, and collect evidence. I don't want all of those people trampling around this hill right here. Who knows what's going to get lost in the sand and the desert at this rate?"

"Yes, I agree." He nods. "I'll go talk to them again. Let's give 'em a few moments though."

The Lanskys' cries are loud and piercing.

I've been doing this long enough to know that there's no point in talking to them now. They're inconsolable. It will take a while for them to speak intelligently again.

Looking down the hill, I can see the deputies leading them back to the house.

"What about them?" Will asks. "Do you think they had something to do with his death?"

"Anything is possible as you know." I nod.

That's the unfortunate thing about our line of work, I think to myself. Anything is possible. All the cruelties of the world, the darkest things that a person can do is something that I find done on an almost regular basis. I don't know how much longer I can put up with this. I want to do a good job and I know that I'm good at it.

Maybe my dad is right. Perhaps, I should have gone to the FBI. Would it be even worse then, if it's like this here in Mesquite County, a quiet desert community, three hours east of Los Angeles.

Why do bad things keep happening here? How much worse are they elsewhere? I look at him once again. I look down at Ricky once again. His frail little body, blue eyes hidden underneath those eyelids. My only hope is that it was a wild animal who did this to him.

Maybe a mountain lion saw an opportunity and attacked. Wild animals don't torture their victims, they kill for food. Occasionally, for play, but it's a matter of survival for them, not pleasure, the way it is for people.

My only hope is that he had a quick death and didn't suffer.

My sadness is that he didn't get to grow up. He didn't get to graduate from high school, get married, have children of his own, pursue his life's passions.

Ricky didn't get to have regrets of old age or the hopes of his youth. He missed out on everything great that life has to offer, but then he also missed out on everything bad.

I take a moment of silence to remember him, this boy that I never knew.

Then I return to my work.

11

CHARLOTTE

The last thing I want to do is go and talk to Mr. and Mrs. Lansky and try to console them during this terrible time, but that's precisely what I have to do. They never made it all the way back to the house. They stopped in front of the garage where somebody provided them with chairs, the kind you take to a kid's soccer game, and the two of them sat, holding onto each other's shoulders crying. They haven't seen his body yet, but they know that their son is dead now. Gone forever.

I take a few moments to gather my thoughts, but it just gets worse. You're supposed to push away this empathy you feel for people in their time of need and be professional, stone faced, and I can do that.

I can detach, be cold and distant, but it doesn't mean that it doesn't affect me. Their sadness, their anger, their disappointment, their absolute devastation, it just crawls inside of me and lives within my heart. I want to be able to help them, but I can't bring back their son. I can bring them justice, whatever that means now, but mostly I can bring them answers.

The next couple of hours are a blur.

We try to talk to them a few times, but each time it goes nowhere with tears erupting and multiple breaks. After a little bit, Will and I decide to give them some space. We can talk tomorrow. We already got their statement multiple times about where they were and what they were doing.

So far, they're not suspects. So far, there hasn't even been a crime. The crime scene investigators collect the evidence around the body, moving Ricky onto a stretcher and into an evidence bag. While he's being moved, I see the gunshot wound and my mouth drops. What little faith I had that this was nothing but an animal attack has now been shattered. Will and I head back to the office, stopping at a drive-through for some coffee and scones.

"You really wanted it to be a mountain lion?" he asks as we talk about the case briefly.

"Of course," I say. "I don't want it to be some bad guy, some awful thing that happened to him, and a mountain lion attack is not that."

"Well, there's a lot of wilderness around here. But the bullet wound changes everything. Where was he shot?"

I point to the lower part of my rib cage.

"Here, I think. We'll hear more from the medical examiner, of course."

"How long do you think the preliminary results will take?"

"I don't know. It's usually about six to eight weeks for an official report, but a preliminary one with her initial impressions and findings can take a lot less time. It will point us in the right direction or at least *a* direction to see where we should go from here."

The day is coming to an end. It's almost closing time. There have been some budget cuts in the department and overtime has to be specially approved. Lieutenant Soderman doesn't want us working on anything outside of normal hours unless absolutely necessary, and in this case, the interviews of the neighbors and the parents will have to wait.

"It's been a long day," Will says. "I need some sleep. I think I'm going to be in by eight."

"Yes, me, too," I say.

I'm tempted to ask him about Erin again, but just as I'm about to, he raises a hand and says, "I don't want to talk about it," as if reading my mind.

"Congratulations on the baby though," I say. "I mean, are you ready to be a father?"

"No, absolutely not. Not even ready to be a husband, but I want to be."

"I think you're going to make a good dad," I say, "and you and Erin have known each other for so long. If it wasn't completely unethical and possibly illegal, it wouldn't be so romantic, would it?"

He rolls his eyes. We bicker back and forth like a brother and sister because we've seen each other through the worst of things. We've never had a romantic relationship because neither of us was really interested. It's not that he's not objectively attractive. It's just somehow we never clicked that way. Plus, I think neither of us wanted to mess up this friendship that we had between us that was so much closer.

"I'm still not sure what you should do about it," I say, "but with the trial--"

"Yes, yes. I know," Will cuts me off. "Like I said, I don't want to talk about it."

"Okay," I say. "I got it."

I get home completely spent, exhausted, and lie down on the couch without taking off my shoes or washing my hands or doing any of the normal things that I usually do when I come back from work.

Dylan is already here. He had called and ordered dinner, and he sits down next to me and pulls off my shoes.

"Thank you," I say, opening my eyes slightly to acknowledge his existence.

"Do I really want to know?" he asks.

I shake my head. "Just a tough case."

"Yes, glad I don't have those."

I smile, giving him a little smirk.

"But actually, I've got to go. The food will be here soon and then I've got to split."

"What are you talking about? I thought you were spending the night and you're off from work?" I ask.

"Yes, change of plans. I'm being sent up north, the mountains near Quail Lake. There's a big fire. It just started. I have to drive up."

"Wow. Really?" I say.

"Yes. I'm sure it'll be out in a little bit. It's too early for full-blown fire season, but they need all the hands they can get."

"But don't you have to like, rush now?"

"No, the local firefighters are there now. I'm just backup. I'm going to have some dinner though, since I'm probably not going to eat anything decent beyond granola bars for two or three days. When we're pushing it hard, things like food and sleep fall to the wayside."

"Oh, I'm sorry." I nod. "I'd love to see you in action."

"Well, with that, you're going to have to go to a big forest fire and look out in the distance and see a row of us holding up hoses, but that's pretty much it."

I smile. "You know you like to downplay what you do, but it's very important."

"No, I know it is and I enjoy it, but the hours can leave a lot to be desired, so can the pay."

"Okay. Let's enjoy this Thai food."

The doorbell rings and he brings in a bag of Styrofoam containers.

"Okay. One rule though," Will says as he cuts open the plastic bag and throws the food into my ceramic bowls, "neither of us can talk about work while we eat. There must be something else that we can say."

I nod in agreement, and I'm about halfway through my Pad Thai before either of us says a word and we burst out laughing.

"Listen, when it's all you can think about, it's all you can think about," I say. "You know how it is?"

"Oh, I do. For sure."

"Well, if we're not going to talk about work, then let's at least watch something funny. Let's watch some fails on YouTube."

"That's a good idea." I nod and give him a kiss on the cheek.

12

CHARLOTTE

D ylan goes home to pack and we say a brief goodbye. Beyond dinner there isn't much time for anything else, not a quickie, nothing but a long kiss goodbye.

We haven't been together long and we haven't talked about the status of our relationship but we're close. I know that he feels for me what I feel for him and that we just can't seem to get enough of each other. That's why I have to work and whenever we have breaks, we always text, call, and try to see each other as much as possible.

"Stay safe," I say, giving him one more kiss before letting him go.

"Don't worry about it. It's going to be fine. All in a day's work."

"Yes, I guess," I say, not quite believing him. "I've never seen you do your job."

"It's not exactly something that people are really invited to. It's more something you flee," he jokes.

"Yes, I know," I say, shaking my head at him. "But you know what I mean."

"Well, for what it's worth, I've never seen you at work either. Never seen you arrest anyone, interrogate a perp, none of that."

"Hah, good one," I say. I pull away from him and wave goodbye just before he pulls me in close for one last kiss.

I LOAD the plates into the dishwasher and clean the kitchen counters. I'm not a very meticulous person, but I do like things clean when I come back from work. Given that it's mainly me and occasionally, me and Dylan, it's not that hard to keep things in order.

Afterward, I head to the bedroom, change out of my clothes and into the most comfortable pair of pajama pants that I have. I take off my bra and put on a t-shirt that's loose but comfortable, but not too oversized, as well as a cardigan that feels as soft as butter.

The night goes by restfully. I was exhausted from complete lack of sleep the last couple of nights, and I fall asleep early and sleep without waking for a good ten hours. In the morning, I hop on the treadmill, do a quick 30-minute walk while reading the news, and then jump in the shower. I let my hair air dry. It's already eighty-five degrees outside, and with a low humidity of the desert, it'll dry in twenty minutes.

When I get to work to do some paperwork, I'm one of the first ones at the station. I like this time best. The buzz of the morning is still somewhere in the distance and now I can catch up on emails and reports without being disturbed by others.

There's a whole lot of paperwork that goes into this job. Everything has to be documented. Every interaction and every piece of evidence has to be filed and organized. That's the stuff that never shows up on TV cop shows.

This is what most people consider the drudgery of their jobs and what makes me incredibly relaxed.

A couple of hours into writing and editing reports, I feel at peace and full of energy. My work phone rings. It's an unfamiliar number. Thinking that it might belong to Kelsey, I answer.

"Hello, Detective Charlotte Pierce. This is Maggie Brayton. I'm a journalist with Mesquite News."

"Uh-huh," I mumble. "What is this about?"

"I'm calling about the body of the boy who was found on his property, Richard Lansky."

"Yes." I nod even though she can't see me.

"I have a few questions about the case for my article."

"Sure. Go ahead."

Getting calls from reporters is pretty common, and usually it falls to me.

The lieutenant hates dealing with the press. He's notorious for his belief that they cause more harm than good, especially when it comes to reporting on true crime. He has very little interest in shows like *Dateline* and *20/20* and cares even less about the people who consume them on autopilot, on channels like Oxygen.

He mildly tolerates the local reporters that we come in contact with, knowing that we need them to get the information out to the public. But he sees them as a useful villain.

Maggie asks me to confirm a few things about what we found and what she heard. Most of it is true but I correct her that we did indeed find the bike, something that we are not keeping private at this time.

"What do you think the cause of death is?" Maggie asks.

"At this point, I can't really say. We're still waiting on the preliminary autopsy report and that's going to take a little bit."

"But can you say whether it's foul play, like somebody murdered him or whether it was just an animal attack?"

"I really can't. No, I'm sorry."

Maggie asks a few more questions, which I happily answer, verifying more facts of the case. Prior to hanging up, she thanks me for my time and I thank her for the courtesy of getting the facts straight from the source.

"Can I ask you one more question?" Maggie asks.

"Yes, sure." I nod.

"As you know, there was another little boy who went missing in Desert Willow. Do you have any idea if his case is at all connected to this one?"

I stop playing with my hair and freeze. Did I hear what I thought I just heard? No, that can't be right.

"What other little boy?" I ask.

MAGGIE BRAYTON IS RIGHT. Only he's not missing, he's dead. His body was found about thirty miles north in the high desert, in the town of Desert Willow early this morning.

He was also six years old and had also been riding his bicycle. When I called the investigators, the deputies on that case, we found a lot of similarities. His body was also covered up, lots of scratches and bruises but no clear evidence of foul play just by looking at him. Same age, same-sex, same manner of death.

When the body was lifted up, they also saw a bullet wound in the lower rib cage, just like Ricky had. I look through my notes of the exact dates of when the two occurred. I interviewed the Lanskys yesterday, May 28th, but he went missing the afternoon of the 27th. May 29th in the morning is when this boy Brian Heller went missing. Exactly two days later.

"When I got to the scene, I saw a dilapidated house that didn't exactly look like a crack den but close to it," the deputy who answers my call says. "The neighbor said that there was a parade of men in and out of that house. One of them was the dad."

"Hmm," I mumble, taking notes.

"According to the mother, the boy was always up early," he continues. "She noticed that he was gone around seven but he had been riding his bike since maybe five fifteen."

"In the morning?" I ask.

"He always woke up really early," the deputy says. "They have two other little kids younger than him in the house. I guess they were crying, maybe woke him up."

"I'm going to drive out there and take a look in person. Okay?"

"Of course, we'll be here probably all day."

I hang up and stare at my notes before taking Will to Lieutenant Soderman's office and filling them both in on the case.

"Desert Willow is thirty minutes away. But I'm not sure if the two cases are related," Will insists.

"It's not just the location," I say. "It's everything at once. They both died under similar circumstances."

"They weren't riding their bikes at the same time of the day," Will says.

"One was in the morning and one was in the evening, but they both went missing and their bodies were found with gunshot wounds."

Will curses under his breath.

Lieutenant Soderman looks at him with disapproval and asks, "Do you really think that the cases are related?"

"I think we should drive up there and talk to them." I shrug. "I'm not really sure but I think it's a little odd that something like this happened when we haven't had anything like this happen before. They're both shot below the rib cage in their backs, their bikes and their bodies were partly buried."

"It's worth having a chat. I'll call up there and tell them you're coming," the lieutenant says. "Hopefully, we can share some information and get this thing solved. There must be some messed up killer who's out there doing something like this."

13

CHARLOTTE

I drive up to Desert Willow by myself. Will has a lot of paperwork to catch up on and tells me that we'll meet up in a little bit. It's all good. I don't mind being alone in the car. In fact, I kind of prefer it.

For work, we're encouraged to not just write down notes but to record them into a device or our phones, whatever is easiest, in order to have the most accurate impressions of what is going on. It's one thing to try to put together a report based on your notes and it's another to walk around the crime scene and make verbal notes of what you're seeing right at the moment.

Over the last few years, I got so used to talking into my phone, using the Voice Memos app, that it actually started to crystallize my thinking. I've noticed how much of an impact it had on me, and I wondered whether I could use the app as a way to journal my thoughts.

Basically, journal out loud.

That's what I like best about alone time on the road. Letting my mind wander, I turn on my voice recorder and let it run through the car speaker system. Sometimes I talk about my day, other times about the past and the complicated relationship that I have with my father and my family in general.

I never have anything planned of what exactly I'm going to say. I just open my mouth, look around, and start speaking. Just as I pull onto Highway 35, going up into the high desert of Mesquite County, I drive past the sea of windmills in front of me all around.

The wide six-lane freeway narrows into three as it splits off with most people heading west toward Los Angeles. I like this road. It's empty and fast and goes through the wide expanse of the desert with nothing but mountains out in the distance on either side. There are some shrubs, but mostly it is sand and sky that fills up the entire view. This is big sky country. Here the world is consumed by it, and that's the way we all like it.

Today the words don't come that easily. I stop and start the recorder a couple of times, practically giving up, but I let it go, forget about it for a few moments. Then, two minutes into it I suddenly say, "I miss her."

Is it possible to miss someone you don't remember ever meeting? Perhaps.

I think I have some memories of my mother, but the thing about memories from when you're two years old is that they're hard to pinpoint as true, accurate, or precise.

Do you remember it because it's your memory?

Or is it something that you remember because you heard your dad describe it or saw it in a picture and had just *incorporated* it into your memory?

I sometimes wonder if this is what it's like to have Alzheimer's; you try to search your mind for a memory, but it just doesn't come. Perhaps you fill it up with other ones and you focus on those instead.

I know that's not fair to my mother, but what else can I do? My mom disappeared.

That's not the right word, especially coming from someone in law enforcement.

My mom had left.

That's more like it. She took off, according to my dad. He tried to find her, but she disappeared for good. Those are his exact words that he delivered to me when I was eleven years old, and I finally had the courage to ask about her.

Over dinner while we were watching TV, I turned to my dad and asked, "Where do you think Mom is, and what happened exactly?"

I planned to ask this question for so long and thought Dad would surely fill in the gaps.

Instead, he turned to me, chewing his pasta, and said, "Ah, she took off, didn't want to be a mom anymore. She left. I looked for her at first, but she was gone."

"Did you look for her? Did the FBI?"

"No."

"What about the police?"

"No, I never reported her missing. She told me she didn't want to be married anymore. She didn't want to be a mom anymore. She's an adult, Charlotte. She has the right to leave and do what she wants, no matter who she hurts, no matter the consequences."

I didn't want to hear that. Not at all. When I tried to talk about it again, Dad shut me down.

For years, I thought it was because he had been hurt. His wife left him with a small child and a demanding job, which didn't exactly make him rich, but then when I grew up, I wasn't so sure.

One day, years later, when I was home from college, I overheard my dad talking to Sherry, my stepmom.

They were in the kitchen eating breakfast, and I was in the pantry. I had come down earlier, but they didn't know that I was there.

"She's dead. You just know these things, Sherry. When somebody walks out on you, you just know."

The way that Dad said that sent chills down my spine.

How could he know for sure that she was dead?

I put that aside because I knew that Dad would never talk to me about it. He'd shut me down a few times already. This topic was clearly off-limits at our regular dinners, but what did he mean by that?

Perhaps Sherry would know, but I never asked her. Sherry and I have a good relationship. Well, decent. She came into my life at a crucial point and she helped me adjust more than I even realized at the moment, at that time, but I was also fourteen. I only lived with her for four years, and she had children of her own, and there were some problems blending the families together.

We see each other for holidays, occasional other visits, but we never talk about anything that important. I know that her birthday party is coming up. She's planning a reunion of sorts soon that I had confirmed that I would attend.

I was thinking of missing it, but I haven't seen Sherry in a couple of months, and we haven't talked on the phone that much either. Frankly, I miss her. She is a good mom. I just wish she had been my mom a little bit longer. Or, maybe if I was a different age so I could connect more.

I was a difficult teenager: moody, self-absorbed, full of darkness and detachment. No one could get through to me. I was unreachable, partly because my mother had left, at the time that I needed her most, and partly because I felt immeasurable guilt over what had happened with Kelsey.

This guilt I couldn't solve, which I couldn't deal with, that I could just bury deep inside of me.

Kelsey's disappearance was still a fresh wound at that time, and I firmly believed that we, and I in particular, was the one who was responsible for the fact that she was gone. Almost every night, my thoughts went to all the horrible things that were happening to her and I stopped sleeping.

I TAKE a deep breath and realize that I'm almost at Desert Willow as I pull up over the mountain onto the flat part of the high desert. We have mountains down in Palm Valley, but they start at sea level. Out here, they start close to four thousand feet and rise higher.

The weather is about ten to fifteen degrees cooler in the summer and the winter. When I look at the temperature gauge, I see that it's seventy-four degrees outside. Perfect.

I turn off my phone and think about how I would've never thought about my mom if I hadn't started talking out loud and letting my words simply flow out of me. This is night and day from sitting in front of the computer screen, staring at the blank page.

What if I tried this with a story? Could I make something up and tell it out loud? Or, would that be different somehow from journaling?

The Desert Willow police station is a new two-story building towering over the valley. There's a parking lot next to it and nothing else for miles. The town itself is rather small, hovering around twenty-five thousand people, most of whom live on properties of two- to five-acre plots. It's a rural community with a few affordable housing condo developments, some new construction builds, but mostly old, two- to three-bedroom homes that are around a thousand square feet.

There's a lot of hustle and activity inside the station and it takes the deputy out front a few minutes to get back to me. I wonder if this is the general tone of the place, or whether that surge of excitement is as a result of the murder case.

Lieutenant Corbett walks up to me and introduces herself. She's young, probably early forties, with olive skin, a short hairdo, and wide-set eyes.

Unlike Soderman who hides in his office to avoid the press, Lieutenant Corbett talks to them with ease, answering questions, doing all of the outreach and public relations that is an expected part of her position.

"You might as well come over and I can just fill you and the FBI in at the same time."

"The FBI?" I ask.

"Yes. After your call, we figured that the more hands we can get on this, the better. Two dead children, same county, very similar circumstances. It could be connected."

I follow her up the stairs and into a back office. A few people join us who don't introduce themselves, and I overhear the lieutenant tell one of her coworkers, "I just wanted to notify the FBI to make sure everything's on the up and up, especially after the fiasco with the missing cases last year. I didn't really expect for them to send anyone so quickly."

"I guess he was in the area," her colleague says. "Hope they don't take over this case."

"It's just him. I don't know if they'll be sending any more people," the lieutenant says. "He seemed pretty cooperative and wanting to work together with all the law enforcement agencies."

"Yes, they got burned by that, too, didn't they?"

I know exactly what they're referring to. There was a case of a missing girl. At first, it wasn't clear whether maybe her father took her, but when she went missing, two other girls went missing as well. There were some issues with the local FBI office, and a couple of agents had quit due to sexual harassment from the higher-ups. They dragged their feet on sending new people out. All three girls were found murdered a week later.

There was a journalist who got a hold of the story, splashed it all over *California Monthly*, which is a magazine that does long exposés on various investigative topics in the state. One month, the lead story was the Prison Fight Club that the guards had organized at San Quentin. The next was this story about the three missing girls and the murderer that the FBI never caught because they were so preoccupied in covering up their sexual harassment case.

We get to the upstairs office a few minutes later, and the FBI agent dressed in a suit stands by the window, looking out at the expanse of Joshua trees reaching their crooked hands toward the cloudless sky.

"Agent Welch, I'd like you to meet Detective Pierce."

"Please, call me Philip," he says, extending his hand.

My breath gets stuck in the back of my throat.

My body recoils away from him.

It's *him*. He's the one.

I recognize him immediately.

14

CHARLOTTE

I know him. I would know him anywhere. His beady eyes, the stubble on his chin. I can practically smell the beer on his breath from that night. Agent Philip Welch extends his hand and smiles that conniving little smile. I pull everything that I have within me and push that feeling of helplessness away.

"Nice to meet you, Charlotte Pierce," he lies through his teeth, pretending that he doesn't know me.

"Didn't we meet at a conference once before?" I ask, the words escaping my lips before I'm really ready. For a moment he looks shaken.

His cheeks flush red. I had called him on it in a however minor way.

"Oh, yes. Yes, of course," he stumbles over his words. The nervousness of that night comes back.

His eyes dart from side to side, but Lieutenant Corbett doesn't seem to notice. A few more people gather in the room with us, and she thanks us all for coming.

"As you know, we called the FBI because we want to have as many hands on deck here as possible," she says, standing in front of a whiteboard.

The lieutenant doesn't hold anything in her hands but is a very natural and confident speaker, addressing the room of people as if she's talking to an individual.

I wish I could focus. Philip's not staring at me, but his mere presence in this room makes me sick to my stomach. It has been a few years now since I've seen him, yet the memories are raw, almost like what he did had just happened.

"This is the little boy in question. His name is Brian Heller," the lieutenant says, showing us a picture of the kid smiling ear to ear, all teeth, wide eyes, eager to start first grade.

The next photo shows his lifeless body lying in the desert partially covered by sand.

She goes over the story that the deputy told me earlier, revealing no additional details. The preliminary autopsy results are still not available, but given the fact it's the second murder in the county and the circumstances are so similar, both autopsies are now going to be fast tracked.

"As I told you, Detective Pierce, we don't know yet if the cases are connected. I'd appreciate it if you would say a few words about your victim."

I stand up and fill them in. I'm not nervous to do this anymore. You list a bunch of facts, dates, names, details, and the few minutes tick by. I feel the room watching me, but it's Agent Welch's gaze that feels like it has the most strength.

Afterward, as we all confer and chat about the cases, we don't make much headway one way or another. We don't know anything yet.

The autopsies are going to be everything. Information about the wounds and the possible weapon as well as other details about what had happened to the victims' bodies will go a long way in helping us determine who had the means and opportunity to be in both places. If the cases are indeed connected.

When I get ready to leave, I hand her my card and ask Lieutenant Corbett to stay in touch, promising to do the same.

"What about me?" Agent Welch asks. "Don't I get a card?"

His blatant arrogance does not take me by surprise.

"You can reach me through the lieutenant," I say quietly.

"Oh, no, let's have as many lines of communication open here as possible," the lieutenant says, oblivious to our tension. "I want to make sure we catch this guy."

I can't very well say no, so I reach into my pocket. When I hand Philip my card, he places his thumb over mine and presses down a little bit, giving me a small wink.

I clench my jaw and do everything in my power not to punch him in the face right there and then.

When I get back to my car, I let out a deep sigh. Not so much of relief or anticipation, but just as built-up energy that has nowhere to go.

I can't work with this guy, I think to myself. He can't be a part of this case.

Staring out at the burnt orange desert, my eyes get a little blurry and I space out.

The knock on the window startles me and I jump.

When I glance up, I see Agent Philip Welch.

I shake my head no, almost like he's a panhandler asking for change on the side of the road, but he knocks again.

"What do you want?" I say through the window, not lowering it.

He points to his ear with his finger almost like he can't hear me even though it's clearly loud enough.

I lower it just slightly, leaving a little crack. "What do you want?"

"I just want to say that I'm looking forward to working with you."

"Well, I'm not."

"You know, you don't have to be so rude. We can have a *working* relationship."

"Um, no, I don't think so."

"Come on, Charlotte. Please."

I start the engine and rush out of the parking lot. I never wanted to see that man again in my life, and here he is walking free, *working an investigation* with me.

And it's all my fault.

I didn't stand up for myself. I made mistakes. I let him off the hook.

I was a young cop who should have known better but didn't. I did the one thing that women often do when they're scared. I hid. I kept quiet and protected the man who hurt me.

I know better now. I should have known better *then*.

15

CHARLOTTE

On the way back home, I try to make sense of what happened. My thoughts, which should be occupied with the two dead boys, are instead distracted and disjointed. I can't stop thinking about the past.

It was years ago at a continuing education conference in Northern California, Sonoma County. I was excited to go. It was my first one, I was only a year out of the academy. I was going to learn all about the latest tactics, weapons, investigative approaches. There was going to be a test afterward, but that didn't matter. I knew how to study.

I didn't have time to drive up, which I would have loved, taking PCH all along the coast to Big Sur and then on up into the wine fields. Instead, I flew because I only had a few days off from work.

I brought a new backpack, pens, notebooks, and a computer, uncertain as to the best way to take notes. This was when I was eager and excited for my work. The conference ended up being a lot bigger than I had anticipated. There were no small rooms, but giant lecture halls full of bored cops forced to do continued education units, which most despised.

The one thing you have to know about cops is that they don't like to study. They like to think of themselves as more doers than anything else. They want to be out there solving real-world problems, and sitting in a lecture hall is something that many find boring and stupid.

I wasn't like that. I always enjoyed learning. I like to read. The easiest way to start learning something new is to listen to a lecture and take in what that person is laying out. That saves so much time over experience. But many don't agree with my thinking.

At that point, I didn't have many friends in the department, a few acquaintances, people I knew from the police academy, but that was about it. I thought that would be a good opportunity to meet new people, maybe get to know some women who could become lifelong friends. I went through periods in my life where I would seek out friendships and then recoil from them, and it was always hard for me to maintain an ongoing relationship.

The days were long, filled with lectures from eight a.m. to six in the evening, with a small break for lunch. Some were more demonstration-based than others, like ones about firearms and tasers and others were a bit mind-numbing due to the quality of the lecturer. One that I found fascinating, despite the presenter, was about decomposition and how long it takes for a body to decompose in various types of ground around California, the desert, swamp, coast, and high alpine areas.

On the third night, I decided to treat myself to a happy hour. I'd avoided drinking until then even though others had not. That night, I found myself at the bar talking to a number of different people from different departments from all over the state. Many were from smaller departments, out east, in the mountains, in the north, and many had questions about what it was like to work for the LAPD with its rowdy reputation, and that was me being rather generous.

I tried to be as diplomatic as possible, talking about the good and the bad, but most people mainly wanted to hear about the bad; the shootings of unarmed civilians, unsolved murders, gang violence, the largest amount of cocaine or heroin or meth that I'd found at one time. My stories weren't that exciting. I was just a deputy on the street and many quickly lost interest, but one didn't. He was a young

FBI agent who was there for some training that overlapped with mine.

Philip Welch was friendly and had a nice demeanor. He'd grown up in San Diego, and he was working in Southern California. I was tempted to tell him about my dad but I didn't want to find out that they worked in the same department or had anything to do with one another, so I kept that part of my story to myself.

I had two drinks, signature cocktails made by the bar staff at the restaurant. Philip invited me to dinner. I had another drink, a glass of red wine, which I nursed all night but about halfway through dinner, I started to feel queasy, tired and we had to cut it short. He offered to help me to my hotel room. I thought nothing of it at first. At this point, I was having trouble walking, stepping one foot in front of another. I had to lean on the wall for support.

When I couldn't find my key card in my purse, he did it for me. When I tried to swipe it the light kept flickering red to green because I couldn't do it in time. After that, the memories become more of a blur.

We were inside my hotel room. Philip was helping me get undressed.

I told him no, but he didn't stop.

He was on top of me. He was holding me down. I kept trying to protest but my arms and legs weren't working.

The scent of his cologne and the beer on his breath made me want to throw up. I felt like I had the flu.

And those piercing eyes...the same ones I saw today in Lieutenant Corbett's office.

16

CHARLOTTE

For the next few days, I keep getting in touch with the medical examiner, pushing her to get me the information as quickly as possible. This is not an official report, but a preliminary one based on her early findings. An official one would be typed-up, signed, and presented to the court. There's a lot more pressure for everything to be right. What I'm looking for are her impressions, some details of what she saw, and how she interpreted the findings.

The official certification of death gives us law enforcement a lot to go on. It includes things like date and time that the victim was pronounced dead, date and time of death, cause of death, manner of death, and additional items like tobacco use and status of pregnancy. If there are injuries, it includes details of those injuries.

The medical examiner reports the underlying cause of death, whether it's due to disease or injury that initiated the train of morbid events leading to the person's death, or the circumstances of the accident, or violence that resulted in the fatal injury. In addition to the underlying cause of death, this section of the medical examiner's report also provides for the entire sequence of events leading to death, as well as other conditions that have significantly contributed to the death.

The cause of death section is designed to list the opinion of the medical examiner. It's a medical opinion and it might vary among different people. That is why a properly completed cause of death section provides an etiological explanation of the type, order, and association of events that resulted in death. The initial condition that starts the etiological sequence is specific if it does not leave any doubt as to why it developed. For example, sepsis is not specific because a number of different conditions can result in sepsis, but death as a result of HIV is specific.

The conditions present at the time of death may be completely unrelated and arise independently of each other. For example, someone could be pregnant or could be using drugs and alcohol at the time of their death but those things are not directly related to the cause of death. On the other hand, the death may result from the combined effect of two or more of these conditions.

The proper completion of that section of the certificate is of utmost importance to the efficient and effective working of a medical-legal investigative system. The cause of death section is completed by medical examiners or coroners. In Mesquite County, it's completed by Dr. Miranda Cowley. She has almost twenty years on the job, got her training at UCLA, and moved out here to take care of her mother, who had retired in Palm Valley.

She had grown accustomed to the place and fell in love with it. Eventually, marrying a man who owned a string of mechanic shops in the valley, and having children.

When I call Dr. Cowley a third time, two days after my initial two calls, she finally answers and gets back to me.

"Sorry, I've just been swamped. I've had a couple of car accidents as well as these two cases. I wanted to have something for you before we started talking."

"Okay, do you have something now?" I ask.

"As you have seen, there are a number of abrasions on both bodies. A few of them occurred after death when the bodies were dragged. I can't say. It looks like the boys had been punched in the stomach a few times, and both of them have black eyes but nothing to the face except for some cuts and bruises. I can't say at this point whether those cuts and bruises were accidental from falling off a bicycle, which is very possible, or as a result of trauma."

"What are you trying to say?" I ask.

"That's not all, they've both been shot by a 22 caliber rifle. The casings were found at the scene, and the bullets match one another. It's the same person, very likely," Dr. Cowley says.

"What does this mean exactly?" I ask.

"He either pulls them off their bicycle, or they get off themselves and he chases them down."

"Can the bruises and the abrasions be attributed to them falling down running away from him?" I ask.

"Yes, it's very possible."

"There were punches to the stomach?"

"Punches or kicks. It's unclear at this point. I have to complete the autopsies, but yes, somebody hurt them very badly and killed them."

"They were kicked or punched before death or after?"

"Before."

"What about sexual abuse?"

She hesitates for a moment, and I hold my breath. So much bad has already happened. I hope that they weren't also sexually abused. Little boys go missing and the people that tend to want to kill them have all sorts of urges and perversions that do not have the greatest outcomes.

"I was surprised, but no, no trauma at all," Dr. Cowley says. "Of course, I can't tell if they were molested or anything like that but they were not raped."

"Okay. That's something. I mean, how rough is it when that's good news, right?"

"There's something else, Charlotte," Dr. Cowley says. "They were shot in the lower rib cage in the back when they were walking away. They likely dropped to their knees and fell. And the way that they were covered up with the dirt and debris, it's almost ritualistic. They were covered up just enough but not buried fully."

"Is there any chance that he tried to bury them but couldn't, like the ground was too hard?" I ask.

"Maybe, but there were no attempts, right?"

I think back, scrolling through my phone for photos of the crime scene.

"No, there are no signs of digging that I saw anywhere near them."

"One option is that he covered them up haphazardly. Maybe planned on coming back for the bodies and digging the graves later but they had been found already," Dr. Cowley says. "The other one is that there were no plans. It was a spur of the moment thing. He used the exact same weapon, did the exact same thing because it just worked out. It was an urge of some sort and not a lot of thought had gone into it."

"I guess that's up to me to find out now. Anything else that you can tell me?" I ask.

Dr. Cowley sighs.

"I'd tell you to look at family members, uncles, male members, but the 22 could be used by anyone. It's a small enough weapon, easy to handle, common around these parts. Often used to shoot squirrels, rats, and rabbits, as you know."

"Were they shot once or multiple times?"

"One time each."

"They died on the spot?"

"Yes, they were shot actually in the exact same place, lower rib cage in the back. The manner of death is as close to identical as you can get if you think about it."

"Yes." I nod, wondering what this means.

I hang up and stare at the blue light coming off my computer screen. People are bustling around me. Some are talking in hushed tones, others projecting into their phones. The guy a few desks over is hunched over his laptop, typing furiously, two fingers at a time. You'd be surprised how few cops can type with their whole hand. I wonder if they'd be faster writing these reports on their phones.

17

CHARLOTTE

When Will and I grab some coffee, I fill him in on the details. We head outside and walk a circle around the park. It's about half a mile but enough to stretch our legs, get some sun. It's ninety-five degrees out, but the heat is dry, and a nice change from the sixty-seven-degree air-conditioned room. The iced coffee goes down nicely as well.

"What does this mean?" he asks. "Wow. So there's somebody here who's shooting little boys, killing them for no reason."

"Not like there is a reason to shoot little boys," I add. "But yes, he's a sicko. I was kind of waiting for a third one to happen soon but it's been two days, and it's either not the right pattern or maybe two was enough."

"We've got to notify the community," Will says. "We've got to do a big press conference, splash it across as many social media sites and newspaper pages as we can, have this take up a lot of ink."

"Yes, I agree. Chances are this person isn't a stranger. Unless it is a stranger, and those are the hardest cases to solve as you know."

He nods.

"Are you going to call Mesquite News?"

"Yes. I have to call them and the local news. We need to have them come to the press conference, do interviews with the parents, that whole thing."

"What do we do in the meantime?" Will asks.

After a quick walk, we head over to Brian Heller's parents' house to interview them one more time about their boy. We had talked to them a couple of times already and unlike what the deputies reported, the Hellers are married and do live in the dilapidated '60s-style house together. The neighbors reported that there are a lot of people in and out from the property, but Samantha Heller explained that they run an Airbnb, and guests can come and stay in their guest house seven days a week. Many are just passing through travelers who stay for a night or two.

She shows us the guest house as no one is there, and she's just cleaning up the bed. It's about a hundred feet away from their main house on their almost one-acre sandy plot with a handful of trees and a beautiful view of a mountain right behind them.

The guest house itself is quite spacious. It's a studio with a king-size bed and a makeshift kitchen with a small dorm-size refrigerator, microwave, plug-in stovetop, and pans and an electric kettle that the guests can use.

"What kind of people come through here?" Will asks.

"All sorts. Sometimes traveling nurses, sometimes families on a budget going to the national park, traveling salesmen. It just varies. It's a small place and we don't charge very much. Ninety-nine dollars a night which is pretty competitive around here."

Her demeanor has changed. It is completely different from when I first met her. Of course, she was distraught at the loss of her child, but the neighbors made it sound like she was a junkie running a crack house.

In reality, Mrs. Heller looks like an overworked mother with a bit of a hoarding problem. She's quite thin and doesn't keep up with coloring her roots as much as maybe others might want her to.

"Your neighbor said that there were a lot of parties here."

"Our neighbors are awful. They hate the Airbnb," Lucas Heller, the dad, says. "They hate that Brian is riding his bike and ringing the bell. They don't like the fact that our dog is barking. You'd think that they'd be used to all that stuff living in this rural area, but they complain about everything."

"The problem is that the neighbors that bought these properties are LA transplants," Sam says. "They moved out here for some peace and quiet, but yes, we do run an Airbnb, and it's registered with the city."

We walk around their property some more.

"They just don't like to see real rural folks, and they don't like the fact that we don't have a garage. Lucas has all of his tools and the junk cars right out there. They think it's creating a bad ambiance. Our visitors don't seem to mind but they do."

I can tell that the animosity between the people in the neighborhood is thick with hatred. At this point, it's hard to know who's telling the truth, but I'm glad that they're talking to us again, and they both seem very concerned about what happened to their son.

"Can you tell me again about what kind of boy Brian was?" I ask.

"Rambunctious. A little hyper. That's why we got him that bike. He was obsessed with it. Rode it for hours, but yes, at home, this house isn't big enough for him and once we had the two other kids, we encouraged him to roam."

"What do you mean by that?" Will asks.

Lucas Heller untucks his shirt, tucks it back in, and straightens out the collar of his flannel shirt on top. He's tan. He's got the tan of a bricklayer. Someone who spends a lot of time outdoors. He's skinny like his wife, wiry even. When I ask him what he does for a living, he says he installs solar panels all around the high and low desert.

Works for Sandpiper Solar.

"I've worked for them for about five years now. They're great. Throw lots of work my way. Always busy."

"You like it?"

"Yes. It pays the bills. Great with flexible schedule. I can help Sam with the kids."

The kids are four and two, and I ask if the four-year-old is going to school anywhere. She shakes her head.

"The daycares and the preschools around here aren't the best. There's lots of incidents of abuse and just neglect so we're opting out for homeschool, but that has challenges of its own as you know."

"Yes." I nod as if I know anything about homeschooling.

"It'd be great to just drop them off somewhere, have the day free to myself, and have them learn things, but we're worried about the quality of care and the expense. We want to expand the house, and that's going to cost a lot. 900 square feet is a little small, and it'd be great to have a garage for the car business as well."

"You have a car business?" I ask.

"Yes, we do. I love old cars so I want to restore them, but I need space and a garage to do that before anyone's going to drop off their 1957 Ford baby over here. I got the carport but it's not the same thing. We're saving up. Brian loved cars," Lucas says. "Just enamored with them. I knew that was going to focus him more. Get him to pay attention and just not be so distracted all the time. It would give him purpose."

"The doctor wanted us to give him ADHD medicine, but I figured if he's not disturbing anyone, we can deal with him here. I don't want to have him medicated," Sam says. "Who knows what happens to their brain chemistry through the years. I don't want him to become a drug addict later on."

Will and I exchange glances. This is the last thing I expected to hear from them. This kind of concern, this kind of thoughtfulness.

We did a couple of interviews already, but they were too distraught. This is the first time we've gotten to know them for real. The feud with the neighbors makes sense and explains why they were so negative about them. Will and I exchange looks and agree that there's nothing really suspicious about them.

Still, we can't rule them out completely. I ask the Hellers about the kind of weapons that they own. They say that they don't have any. That would be believable in Palm Valley, but up here in the high desert where people live far away from one another in a rural setting, it's a hard ask. Still they insist that they don't have a gun registered in their name and don't have one at all. We're forced to take that at face value. Plus, no weapons were found in their home when the deputies conducted the initial search.

Just as we're about to walk out, someone pulls up to their property. It's a white Toyota Corolla. At first, I think it's a friend of theirs, but as soon as he gets out, everything within me begins to tremble.

18

CHARLOTTE

He's back. As soon as I see him, everything within me tightens up. I look over to the car door to see if maybe I can still make it there without him noticing, but it's too late.

I can't be seen running.

He smells fear.

He can probably taste it.

No, the best thing to do is to put on a brave face and by that, I mean, one that makes me look like a cold stone bitch. I cross my arms, widen my stance, broaden my shoulders, almost preparing myself for impact. Even though I know that he would never punch me out here in the open being the coward that he really is.

The smug look on his face makes me feel nauseous. Philip brushes his hair back. It's much shorter now in that crew cut, that's popular with a lot of law enforcement. While Will looks the other way, he gives me a wink and knowing kind of smile where he's challenging me, telling me exactly what he thinks of me and the fact that he's not afraid.

Why would he be? I let him get away with it all. I didn't press charges, I didn't push. I didn't tell anyone.

If he committed any more assaults after me, I'm probably partially responsible for not coming forward.

When you don't tell anyone at first, the shame just builds and builds and after a while, you feel like you're as guilty for what he has done to you as he is.

But that's not true. From the outside looking in, I know that Philip's a predator, but I also know that law enforcement can't do anything without people coming forward.

We need proof. We need people who are willing to stand up and tell the court that this person did something messed up and I'm going to call him on it, no matter what it costs me career-wise or otherwise.

I didn't do that and so he's here. This is a small desert community where two boys disappeared and were found murdered and the FBI is here to offer their resources.

Will walks over to shake Philip's hand while I take a moment to look at my phone and buy myself some time.

"Charlotte, this is Special Agent Philip Welch."

"Yes, we've met. How are you doing?" I say with a slight nod.

Philip extends his hand. I hesitate. Will glares at me. It's a well-known fact that cops are not happy when their territory is stepped on by higher-ups like ATF, FBI.

Will thinks that it has something to do with that. I'm annoyed that this case is getting taken away by the bigger guys, but he doesn't know the truth. Luckily at that moment, Lieutenant Corbett comes over, interrupting us, and shakes hands with Philip. She quickly fills him in and thanks him for coming.

Apparently, she was the one that had called in order to expand the resources of the department.

"We're just worried that this could become something worse, something more complicated," she says, dancing around the words serial abductions, serial disappearances, and of course, serial killer.

Two dead under very similar circumstances definitely points to that.

Statements have to be made to the press to make the public aware that someone is on the loose.

"The more resources we can have working on this together, the better," Lieutenant Corbett says. "I really appreciate your cooperation and reaching out."

Philip smiles that plastic, nonchalant smile of an actor, endorsing a product that he could not give two craps about. When Philip stays behind with the lieutenant, I see an opportunity to take off.

"I've got to go. I have to get back to all this work," I turn to Will.

"What are you talking about?" He snaps. "What could be more important than this?"

"Listen, we took some statements. This is going to be between the FBI and the lieutenant here."

"I don't know what you're doing," Will mutters, shaking his head.

I head toward my car and a few moments later Will walks up to me. Luckily I parked slightly to the side, far away from Philip's vehicle and the rest of the cars giving us a semblance of privacy.

"What's going on? Do you know him?" Will can read me.

Sometimes I feel like he knows things about me that I can't know about myself.

"I'll tell you later."

"No, tell me now. What's going on? You're acting so odd."

"That guy is bad news. Okay? I don't want him working on this case, I don't want him working with us."

"Why? How do you know him?"

"We have a past."

"You dated and, what, he didn't call you?"

"Please. Do you really think that I'm so petty? I've had plenty of guys not call me and I've ghosted plenty in return. This isn't anything personal."

I hesitate for a moment considering the fact that this isn't exactly true. It's about as personal as it gets.

"Tell me what's going on, Charlotte. I'm your partner. If you tell me that I shouldn't trust him, I won't trust him, but you have to tell me why."

"I can't. It's a long story. I'll tell you later."

"Later when? Tonight?"

"Fine. Let's get some food after work."

"You promise?"

I nod. "Yes, of course."

19

CHARLOTTE

The promise was made casually, but not insincerely.

Will stays behind with the Hellers while I head back and spend the next few hours filling out reports back at the station. After work, we head out to grab a quick bite of Thai food.

"How's Erin doing?" I ask Will as we put in our order at the walk up window and sit down to wait for it to come out.

We each pay for our own food. I get a can of Sprite, something I haven't had in years. It reminds me of school when I used to survive on these things, unbeknownst to my dad.

We sit across from one another in plastic chairs with our food on trays and paper-like plates. He's waiting for me to tell him what happened.

"Listen, I'm only here to talk about one thing," Will says, brushing his hands through his hair.

Pointing his chin downward, he looks up at me through his brows.

"How's Erin?" I ask again.

"She's good. Pregnancy's making her sick, but we're excited and happy."

"Good. I'm really happy for you," I say with the utmost sincerity.

Will is one of my closest friends. Unlike other friendships, things have never been complicated or messed up with him. We've given each other space but now he wants to get close. He wants to know the one thing that I really don't want to share.

Recently it seems all of my secrets are coming to the surface. The situation with Kelsey and all of my old lies. Now Philip has shown up out of nowhere, taunting me, flaunting his power.

Maybe telling Will the truth is the answer.

"Philip and I met at a conference and had dinner," I start.

"I figured something romantic had happened."

"Listen, I'm not a nun tucked away in some convent. I live my life. I meet guys. I go out with them, sleep with some, and the majority aren't anything worth remembering. So what?"

"Listen, I didn't mean anything by it. You know that. I'm the last person to judge."

"I know," I admit. "I just felt that judgment that I guess I feel from a lot of people and I'm just sick of it."

"I understand. But tell me what happened with Philip."

"I went to a conference for work in Sonoma County. It was my first year on the job. The days were really long. You know how those conferences just run into the night, and I met him there. He was there for a similar thing for the FBI. I guess they put everybody in the same hotel, just different meetings. I had a drink with him. I didn't feel good afterward. I woke up in my hotel room passed out."

The words come quickly at first, then slowly. I want to include all the details about how crappy I felt, how lost, confused, but the law enforcement part of me goes on autopilot.

"He was on top of me," I continue. "That's all I remember. Afterward, when I confronted him, he threatened me. He said that if I ever went to anyone, they would do a drug test and they would find that I wasn't just on a date rape drug."

"What did that mean?" Will asks, his mouth agape.

"He meant that they would find heroin in my system, too. I was shocked. I took an at-home test. One of those you can buy at the pharmacy and sure enough, it came back positive. He had drugged me with this cocktail. As you know a lot of people use date rape drugs for fun recreation like, 'Ooh, let me pass out and see what happens. Live life on the edge.' He was going to tell people that I was one of those women."

"I'm so sorry," Will says.

"I had no gun on me obviously and there was blood in my panties and that's how I knew that he had raped me. My whole body was hurting. He had used something besides his dick. I even came close to making a report, but then I saw him talking to a local captain and being all chummy with the higher-ups at the conference.

"He was older and more experienced. He was in the FBI! I was worried about the positive drug test and what it would do to my record and to my career. I was just humiliated, and so I didn't report it. I decided to keep silent because I was a coward I guess."

"No, because you're a victim," Will says, reaching over and touching me. The moment that his hand presses against mine, I recoil.

I had told the story with my mind in the bubble like I was telling it to him but not really. Like I was talking to myself, trying to still make sense of it all, but suddenly it's all different.

He's here. I'm here.

There are plates banging in the background, people coming in and out. A fast food place around dinnertime is not exactly quiet. A kid is crying somewhere in the distance.

"Do you want to go somewhere else? Somewhere more private?"

"No, it's actually fine here. I feel like I can blend into the background, not stand out so much."

"I'm really sorry that this happened."

"Yes, me, too." I nod.

"This is the first time you've seen him since?"

"Yes, but I guess he knew where he was coming because he was prepared. I saw him earlier at the station. He was all smug and full of himself, and I just know that he did it to other girls. He thinks he's unstoppable, and now, what can I say? Now I just look like some person holding a grudge."

"No, you're a victim coming forward years later," Will says. "Did you get any tests at that time?"

"No. I should have gotten a rape kit. I should have gotten an STD test done at a hospital, something, but it's like I covered up his crime in order to protect myself, my stupid career."

Will reaches over to touch my hand but I pull away. Our food is getting cold, but we don't reach for our forks.

"You have to understand. This was before the Me Too movement. I didn't think anyone would believe me. I was so embarrassed. I was there for work and it was like he brought my whole existence down to just being somebody to use and abuse like I didn't matter."

"What do you want to do now?" Will asks.

I shrug. "I don't know. I have to work with him. I don't have that many options."

"I mean, you could work with him, but what about making a report *now*?"

"I'm not sure that's going to do anyone any good. There's always going to be suspicions and then he'll be out. He'll be on alert as well. I think it'd be better if

I just waited for the right opportunity to get him and get my revenge."

"What do you mean by that?"

"Don't worry. I'm not going to kill him if that's what you're thinking," I roll my eyes, "though he deserves that."

Will smiles casually at me. I can tell that he's still worried. I reach over and touch his hand.

"Will, you don't have to worry. I'm fine. Everything's fine, but yes, I'm going to plot my revenge. It's nice to think about whether or not I get it."

"You have to make him pay for this."

"But how?"

"I don't know yet, but we can try to find a way; we can try to catch him. Maybe he's doing this to other people."

"I'm pretty sure that he's been doing it for a long time. Proof is a little harder to get. Let's just do this. Let's just work on this case, figure out who did this to those two little kids. If the FBI wants to help and put their resources into this, then fine. I'm only happy to accept it. I have no idea what kind of agent he is. Maybe he's decent. The resources are still going to be helpful. I'm going to try to work with him for the greater good. If anything else comes out of it, I'll be there to watch him, but I don't know what else I can do."

"I understand." Will nods. "That's probably the best way to do it."

We finish the rest of dinner talking about nothing and everything. I try to change the topic to Erin, and he's happy to oblige. They had gone to a couple of OBGYN appointments. I see how excited he is to be a father. The past still looms however, but I don't bring it up.

The court case is ongoing against the person who killed Erin's ex-husband and his new wife. She's called to be a witness, and so is Will since we officially worked the case.

The prosecutor is going to prepare both of us and then Erin separately on the kind of questions that can and probably will be asked. I'm pretty certain that if they were at all irresponsible about spreading information about their relationship, the defense attorneys would have that in their back pocket.

I don't know any more about that than Will and I just hope that no one else does either. I don't bring it up at dinner. I want to leave this on a good note. We've talked enough about bad stuff to last us a lifetime. For now, I want to support my friend on his newfound journey to fatherhood.

20

CHARLOTTE

The following day when I get to the office, Jen Applegate, one of the Lanskys neighbors, is waiting for me at my desk. She had refused to talk to any of the deputies or anyone besides me, and Will isn't in the office yet.

Normally, I like to ease into my day, get some caffeine running through my veins, but I don't have the luxury of that this morning.

Jen is a sturdy woman in her fifties dressed casually in a Pacific Crest Trail shirt.

"How can I help you, Mrs. Applegate?"

"We have some cameras set up outside our house and I was looking through them. I saw a man leaving the property through the back road. A shadowy figure."

"Great," I say.

"This was the camera that my husband had set up recently so your people didn't see it. I forgot all about it. It has the other angle on the property."

She pulls it up on her phone and shows me. The footage is indeed grainy. The man is dark and far away, an adult who is in his thirties to fifties riding a motorcycle, probably a Harley. The dates and times match up.

"This is the middle of the day. Why would it be so dark?" I ask.

"It's not really dark. It's just placed in a bad location and sometimes the light catches it in a weird way. I'm going to move it after this but I wanted to show you."

"I appreciate you coming in. Really."

She nods. I wonder if she has something else to say. I give her a little bit of space. Sometimes, it's in the pauses and in the quiet moments when the truth emerges.

"I want you to know that the Lanskys are very nice people," she says quietly. "They had nothing to do with this."

"Oh? Can you tell me a little bit about them?"

It's a little bit unusual for her to come forward and say something like this, especially given the fact that no one stated that the Lanskys were suspects in this at all, but I want to give her as much leeway to speak as freely as possible.

"His parents had nothing to do with this," Mrs. Applegate says, cracking her knuckles. "They are the kindest people, and they loved that kid. I know that you're looking at them as the suspects and you just couldn't be more wrong."

"Yes, I understand," I say. "Why don't you tell me more about them?"

At no point did I ever tell her that we were looking at the parents as suspects, but she had probably seen at least one or two crime shows to believe that.

"Danny and I--"

"Mr. Lansky?" I ask.

She nods. "We go climbing a lot. We both love to hike."

"Pacific Crest Trail," I point to her shirt, "did you ever do that?"

She nods.

"Tried three different times, made it as far up as Yosemite but should have started in my twenties instead of my fifties. It's hard to carry that big pack for so long for all of those days, especially if your bones are getting old, but I'm going to try again next year."

I smile.

"There's nothing like spending days and days out in the wilderness, just you and your thoughts and your pack and no other worries in the world."

"I like to hike, too, but never did many overnight trips. Just a little bit of car camping here and there," I say.

"You should let go of that car, those possessions. Just walk out in the wild. There's nothing like it."

"So, is that what you and Danny have been doing?"

"No, not at all. He's a climber. He goes up to the national park. He boulders up there and then comes back. He and Meredith are very close. She used to climb a lot, too, but she got hurt. Her back hasn't let her do it much since. So now he does it by himself. You've been to her house, right? She's an amazing painter."

"You mean she does all of that art herself?"

"Yes. She made all the paintings and installations herself over many years. They tried to have kids for years. Thought that it wasn't in the cards for them and then suddenly Ricky came along. He was a blessing. Everyone was happy for them."

She hesitates, inhaling deeply to stop a wave of emotion.

"What do you think happened?" I ask.

"I don't know. This stranger on the Harley is probably as good of a guess as any."

I sit here and wait for her to say something else, but she just lets her words dangle.

"Have you and Danny ever had a relationship?" I ask.

She recoils in shock. It seems to be the most obvious question, but she looks like it's a surprise.

"No, of course not. My husband has multiple sclerosis and we've been living next door to the Lanskys for years. It's one of the reasons I like to hike. It's a lot to take care of him, and a couple of months off on my own just gives me the opportunity to clear my head. He has help, of course, when his sister comes to visit. Danny and I have a lot in common, but we've never been romantic. We are both too happy in our relationships for anything like that."

"Okay," I say. "Well, thank you for the video, and I'll let my CSI people know about this. Maybe they can get to the bottom of it."

"Thanks. He was a little bright light in our lives. I loved watching him grow up."

"What about your kids?" I ask.

She shrugs. "They're grown. We had them younger. No grandkids though. Too busy with careers, school, and being single. I have three. They're all in their 30s."

I nod.

"Kind of like you. Do you have kids?" she asks.

"I don't. No," I say.

"Too busy with work?"

I shrug not wanting to go into the details of my personal life.

"A child is not just someone to come home to, but someone to share your life with. They can be a lot of work. That's what people seem to complain about a lot, but they're actually a lot of fun."

She's not one of those people that needs to be asked to leave twice. Truth be told, I like Jen Applegate. There's a directness to her that I appreciate, a kind of a no-nonsense approach to life. It's a nice change of pace.

I make some notes on the video of the conversation and then send it over to the CSI team. I will update the lieutenant and Will when I see them.

Right after my lunch break, I stop by the Lanskys once again just to have another chat with them. I look at the pictures of six-year-old Ricky all over the walls, and I pay close attention to the Southwestern artwork that fills the rest of the house. I ask Mrs. Lansky about it, and she confirms that she has made almost ninety percent of the pieces here.

"I picked up art late in life, but it's such a nice release. It just keeps my mind occupied," she says. "It keeps me distracted, I guess. Sometimes I'll listen to some podcasts. Sometimes I'll watch something on TV. Sometimes I'm just alone with my thoughts, nothing but me and the paints, the drawing, the mats, the crayons. I've been trying to do some pottery as well, so I'm learning a whole bunch of new techniques."

Something in her changes when she talks about her art. It's like her mind flips over and she's able to be somewhere else.

"So, do you sell these?" I ask.

"Oh, no. I used to teach math at a community college and my husband still does. He's a professor."

"Hmm-mm," I say.

"Yes, so he earns us enough money to live on and have a nice retirement, and now art is all I do besides raising Ricky."

Suddenly, it's like she remembers. Tears well up, and her face cracks in pain.

"We're going to find who did this," I say.

She nods but doesn't seem to believe me.

For a second, I wonder if she knows who did it.

"I just want him back," Mrs. Lansky says, biting the inside of her mouth and looking up at me, her eyes full of tears. "Of course, I want to know who did this, but that's not going to bring Ricky back, is it? He's gone."

21

CHARLOTTE

When the pain seems to become unbearable, Mrs. Lansky excuses herself and goes to one of the bedrooms. I'm glad that I have some time alone with her husband.

I ask Mr. Lansky about his work. He says he's been teaching math for almost twenty years now. He likes it. He likes being a teacher. He enjoys the college. He likes that he has time to climb.

"It's a job I can do on autopilot at this point, been doing it long enough." He shrugs. "I tried to teach Ricky about numbers but he has always been a letters guy. You tell him a story and he'll be there with you for ages. I try to explain to him about addition, subtraction, his eyes just glaze over and it's like he doesn't care. I'm sure he would have learned, he just wasn't obsessed with it like I was as a kid."

"Was that a problem for you?" I ask.

"No, not at all. I have a wife who taught math and didn't really care about it. That's why she's doing art now. Sometimes you're just good at something and you can do the job, but that doesn't mean your heart is in it. Ricky should have been able to do anything he wanted, and that bastard took that away from him."

"We're going to do everything in our power to find him," I say and mention the guy on the motorcycle.

"You saw the video?" Mr. Lansky asks. "Could you make out the license plate or anything?"

"No, I couldn't. I'm sorry," I say. "CSI has it now. Maybe they'll be able to work something out. I wanted to ask you a little bit about your relationship with the Applegates."

"Yes, they're our close friends."

"And Jen said that you and she go hiking together?"

"Climbing." He shrugs. "She's not much of a climber, but she wanted to learn at one point so we went together. I'm not much of a hiker the way she is. Long-distance stuff, no thanks. Sleeping on the ground in a tent is not my favorite. I did it plenty in my twenties and thirties, and I'm just getting too old for that stuff. But Ricky was really into it. He loved camping. I was going to do it with him."

Mr. Lansky looks away from me. His face contorts as grief washes over him and he can't keep the pain from escaping its depths. Grief is a wave that sweeps over you but not in any regular intervals like a tide. Instead, it comes as a surprise, a tsunami.

"I'm sorry, I need a minute," Mr. Lansky says, pulling away from me. When he gets a hold of himself, he focuses on the logistics.

"We're having the funeral tomorrow. I don't know if I should have invited law enforcement."

"No, not at all, but I do have to say that we would like to attend just to see who's there, keep an eye on things."

"What do you mean by that?" he asks.

"Well, it's a memorial service as well, right?"

He nods.

"Sometimes people who do this, they're so messed up that they want to revel in what they have done. They want to see people's pain. It's not a guarantee, but I have a suspicion that the person who did this may come to the memorial service, pay his respects, and to watch your pain, revel in it, pat himself on the back."

Mr. Lansky's deep blue, piercing eyes glare at me.

"Unfortunately, that's true. We're going to have some deputies there and we're going to keep track of who shows up, who doesn't. We plan to compare the guest list to the memorial and the funeral service of the other little boy up in the high desert."

"God, I'm so sorry about that." Mr. Lansky shakes his head.

"I can put you in touch with the family. Maybe you two can offer each other some support."

"I guess." He nods. "I'm not one for something like that though. I appreciate everyone coming around and asking me questions and offering their condolences, but to be honest, I just want to be left alone. I want to grieve for Ricky on my own. I don't want to just constantly be supporting other people in their pain. You know what I mean?"

I nod. The truth is that I know a lot about how he feels. I'm the same way. I have talked to a therapist a few times, but that's different from talking with friends.

When I shared that with the therapist, she said that I don't want to inconvenience the people I know so I don't feel comfortable opening up. She was right about that.

"Okay, I just have one more question," I say. "It's actually not about Ricky."

He waits for me to explain.

"Your relationship with Jen? Did you two ever have anything more than that?"

"No, never."

"And your spouses didn't feel uncomfortable about you two camping together?"

"Well, we don't go camping together. Just a couple of trips out to the national park to climb boulders. It's hardly anything."

I nod and look down at the floor.

"You don't believe me?" he asks.

I tilt my head slightly to the side and ask, "What makes you say that?"

"Just the way that you're looking at me. I've never cheated on my wife, never would. She has some medical issues now. That doesn't change how much I love her. Jen and I happen to have something in common, so what? I wasn't out there hiking with her on the Pacific Crest Trail. We just shared a ride to climb some boulders the way friends do. Her husband has a lot of issues, too."

"Okay," I say. "I believe you."

"It doesn't seem like it, but whatever," he snaps.

If nothing else I have to believe them unless I hear something different from either of them.

As I walk out, I walk past a pile of baskets and baskets of flowers near the front entryway. Condolences. Regrets. I wonder if these flowers are offering them a semblance of support or if they want to toss all of them in the trash as reminders of what they have lost.

When I get to the car and just before I return to work, I get a call from an unknown number. I'm tempted to let it go to voice mail but not knowing who else could be calling me or what it could be about, I answer.

"I'm from the California Fire Department and I'm looking for Charlotte Pierce."

My throat closes up and I can barely confirm that it's me.

"I would like to notify you as the emergency contact for Dylan Ferreira that he has been hurt up in the Mesquite County mountains. He was taken to the local hospital at Quail Lake to treat his burns."

"Hurt how? What happened?"

"There was a hotspot. The fire surrounded them and, unfortunately, his partner perished. I shouldn't have mentioned that." The woman's voice breaks up. "We're all very distraught over what happened. If you would like to see him please come up to the Quail Lake Hospital. He should be here for the next few days, and I'm sure that the doctor would like to talk to you about pending medical decisions."

I want to ask her so much more but she says that she has to go. I can tell that she is getting worked up and is unable to hold back her tears. I stare at the phone until the screen goes black.

22

CHARLOTTE

I head straight up to Quail Lake to see Dylan. I make a few calls on the way up to account for work, and mostly to pass the time and not to be alone with my thoughts about all the things that might or might not have happened.

He's alive at least, I say to myself to try to calm myself down. But there's so many different ways to be alive.

How bad are the burns?

How bad is the recovery?

How hurt is he *really*?

There's a strong possibility they might not tell me anything. I'm not a family member, wife, not even a fiancée. I don't know how strict they are in those policies, but at least I am an emergency contact and I hope that's enough for them to let me see him.

Quail Lake is a quaint little mountain community up in the pines above the high desert. My ears pop as I drive up over six thousand feet. The creosote bushes slowly morph into green shrubs and then towering pine trees. In the winter, they get snow here and it's a wonderland. There's one ski resort, a couple of different slopes around which all winter and summer activities are centered.

The town itself is small, about fifteen thousand permanent residents, but the tourists come from all over Southern California, making it a popular and somewhat upscale mountain community.

I've been here a few times, stayed in a motel, a lodge, and an Airbnb, but I've never been to the hospital. It's a small community hospital kind of like the one up in the high desert, but even less fancy. The ceilings are low, the people are very friendly, and there's a small parking lot out in the back, hardly filled. The waiting room is sterile and nondescript. There's nothing fancy about it, no floor-to-ceiling windows, no marble tiles, not like the wealthy hospitals in LA.

There are a number of people dressed in fire department uniforms. Not the heavy firefighting ones, but t-shirts with the emblem, people covered in soot and sweat. I walk up to one of the older gentlemen and ask if he knows where Dylan Ferreira is.

"And you are?"

He rubs his forehead with the back of his hand and a little bit of dirt smears along with the sweat.

"I'm Detective Charlotte Pierce," I say automatically, and then realize that I've given him my title as well and this is more of a personal matter.

"I'm actually his girlfriend, his emergency contact," I clarify quickly. "They called me that he was in an accident."

"Yes, of course. Nice to meet you, Charlotte. I'm Gabe Khan, his supervisor. Just popped in here myself to see how they're doing."

"Can you tell me what happened, or how he is?"

"Dylan's in critical care. He and his partner-- he was one of the guys responding to a blaze up here. His partner was actually one of the people that he was with who got killed."

"What happened?" I ask.

"Burns and inhaled smoke, but that's pretty common, they're not always considered fatal," Gabe says. "Doctor is saying that it's probably a cardiopulmonary arrest during suffocation, which was a result of exhausting his compressed air supply while fighting the fire and due to the fact that his face mask was still in place."

"What does that mean exactly?"

"His air tank ran out," Gabe says.

"The fire had surrounded them. You're always supposed to be moving backward, but something must have happened that those procedures weren't followed."

"What about Dylan, exactly?" I ask.

"Dylan had smoke inhalation and has some burns. He's no longer critical. I talked to him."

"You did?"

"Yes, they're managing the pain. The burns aren't too terrible. Doctors are saying that he's going to be out of the hospital in two to three days."

"Oh, that's a relief," I say, letting out a sigh.

"Yes. He got really lucky."

"I'm really sorry about his partner."

"Me, too, but it can happen to any of us. Wildfires are dangerous things to fight. Unfortunately, they're just getting worse and worse every year."

A nurse comes out and I ask her if I can go see Dylan. She walks me over to the desk where I put in my name, show my ID, and fill out all the appropriate paperwork. Afterward, she tells me that I have half an hour and after that they want him to rest.

When I walk in, Dylan's eyes are closed. I can't tell if he's sleeping or not, but the door makes a little noise and he opens them. A smile pulls over his face immediately.

"Hey, what are you doing here?"

"They called me. They said that you were in the hospital, that something bad happened. Of course, I'm here." I rush over to him and hug him.

No burns on his face or chest. Just a little bit on his arms. He coughs a lot when I hug him, still struggling from the smoke inhalation. One of his arms has a cast on it.

"Are you okay?" I ask.

"Yes, just minor damage."

"What happened?"

"We were over closer to the lake. It seemed like a safe place. We were trying to get the fire away from one of the residential homes there, one of the big ones. It wasn't well protected. There's a bunch of incendiary pine needles all around the property and then a gust of wind came through and the fire suddenly shifted direction and connected with a bigger part of it across the way. I don't know exactly what happened but luckily it was just the two of us there. We tried to fight it off but we were being surrounded. The fire was making a circle."

I fight back tears.

"That's the most dangerous thing that can happen in a wildfire when it surrounds you completely in a circle and there's nowhere to go," Dylan continues. "You lose access to water supply. I was wearing a mask, so was he, of course, but something happened, then he passed out. Luckily the wind shifted again and gave me a little bit of an opening so I jumped through the flames. I tried to carry him out, burnt the crap out of my arm, and all up and down here."

He opens a little bit of his blanket exposing his leg and I see that his body is all bandaged up.

"Don't worry, it doesn't hurt." He smiles.

"Yes, I'm sure that's why there's a morphine drip attached to you. Isn't there?"

"It's not morphine, exactly." He smiles. "The opioids are doing their job. The worst thing is when they are changing the dressing. That hurts like a son of a bitch."

"I'm so sorry, Dylan." I take his hand.

"I'm just really happy you're here. I'm glad they called you."

"Well, you did make me your emergency contact." I smile.

"I know. Well, I missed you so I figured this would be a good opportunity for us to hang out again."

I laugh and so does he. For a moment, we forget that we're in the hospital together and it feels just like back home. From the looks of it, it's going to be a long recovery.

"Folger's dead, isn't he?" Dylan asks after a moment.

I shift my eyes to meet his. I wonder if I should lie, keep his hope alive, but for what? He's not in such a dire situation that he's totally hopeless. He's totally lost hope. He just wants to know about his friend. "Yes, Gabe said that he had a heart attack."

"Oh, crap. That's probably why he passed out."

"Why would he have a heart attack?"

"It can happen from stress, that kind of thing, but Folger had other issues."

"What do you mean?"

"They're probably going to find it in the system, but he's a pretty heavy meth user. He worked--"

"Like methamphetamine?"

"Yes. Look, I'm just sharing this with my girlfriend, right? You're not going to get the DEA over here investigating the firefighters are you?"

"No, of course not," I say. "Now, tell me what you're talking about."

"We work a lot of hours, like a lot. Folger was in debt. He had two kids he had to support, two different families. Got the moms pregnant at the same time. They weren't too happy about that and went to court. He got caught using drugs before, was put on suspension, but he's an addict. He needed to go to rehab, which he couldn't afford, and he had to work fewer hours, which he couldn't do either. So it was kind of an open secret in the department that he liked to get high."

He takes a pause before continuing.

"There are a few others that do, too, but there are consequences to that, that are worse for firefighters than others. This is a very demanding job. Requires a lot of strength and conditioning, and you don't get a lot of sleep. I'm not just here talking ill of the dead. Not at all. I'm just trying to tell you the reality of what happened. You of all people know what happens when you do meth for a little too long."

"Yes, it's terrible for your heart, let alone everything else."

"He just kept saying he was going to quit. He didn't. I hope it's a lesson to all the other stimulant-obsessed people in the department," Dylan adds. "Maybe it's the drugs I'm on right now, but it just makes me angry that the thing is that they put everyone's life in danger. We have to depend on them for help. We have to believe that they're going to save us if something were to happen, but the truth is that they could just have a heart attack on you at any moment and pass out, and then you are the one that has to risk your life to save them."

"This is a big problem, a lot of people doing this?"

"Yes. A lot more than you think. It's the crazy hours. After a while, you need a pick-me-up. You get into your late 40s or 50s. You want to work a little less. You don't want all that stress like you craved when you were younger. He's no different, I'm no different."

"What are you saying?" I ask. "Do you use meth, too?"

"No, no. Never. But I drink too much sometimes. I used to smoke cigarettes and it took a while to quit. Now, every time I have a long shift, I want to smoke again. I don't have half the stresses these people do.

My coworkers do. Drama with ex-wives, ex-girlfriends, kids to support."

I let him talk because while he's talking to me, it sort of feels like he's also talking at me like I'm just a springboard, a person here to listen, nothing else.

"That's probably why I never got serious with anyone since my wife. That's why I was always so uncertain about having kids. Just wasn't sure where they fit into my life. I felt bad enough leaving my dog at home, let alone a kid with all their activities and after-school things. You want to be relaxed to spend time with them. You want to be able to be a rock when they're having a hard time, but you can't do that if you're having a hard time yourself. You can't do that if you're completely out of control, exhausted, and substance dependent. Of course, meth is an extreme case of that, but there are other substances that do the trick."

Dylan sneezes and winces. A nurse comes in and asks what level of pain he thinks he has. He says a four. By the looks of it, it looks more like an eight. She lets him up his dose a little bit and then tells me to leave.

"Next time I can come in after you get some rest, okay? I'll be waiting outside." He nods, closes his eyes, and turns away.

"He's trying to be brave for you," the nurse says, "but he's in a lot of pain. The burns are going to hurt for a while."

"Can he walk?"

"A bit. There are burns on the front of his legs up and down, as well as on his arms, his chest, and the left side of his body. Some are worse than others, but they're all going to take a long time to heal. Sleep and rest and time passing are really all we can do besides managing the pain."

"How long do you think he'll have to stay in the hospital?" I ask.

"Can't be sure, two or three days," the nurse says. "But it's going to be a long recovery at home. He will need help and maybe even a nurse."

I hadn't considered that.

"There's the changing of the bandages, managing of the pain, just making food for him, water, taking him to the bathroom. He'll need someone to actually do that."

"Oh, wow," I say.

"If it's not something you can handle, or the family can handle, then there are places that he can be sent to where they can help him recover."

"How long will that take?"

"A month, or two? He has serious injuries here."

"What about his job?"

"Definitely off for any foreseeable future. Burns are not like broken limbs or other things. There's a whole recovery state for them. Skin does turn over, but it depends on how long it takes.

"I've explained all this to his parents already. If you want to talk to them, put together a plan that would probably be ideal. I'll let you know when you can go see him again."

23

CHARLOTTE

Time passes slowly in the hospital. Occasionally, you look up and it's a couple of hours later, and another time you look up and only a minute has passed, but you can't tell the difference.

Some people don't eat or drink when they get stressed, but I have the opposite reaction. It's a combination of boredom, anxiety, and uncertainty that drive me to the vending machine. As soon as I've talked to the nurse, and with the anticipation of meeting Dylan's parents building, I disappear down the hallway for some alone time. When I spot the vending machine full of M&Ms, chips, crackers, and Skittles, I can't pull away. Sweets and carbohydrates have always been my go-to place when the world gets too much.

On one hand, everything that Gabe and the nurse have told me is a relief. Dylan is okay. He's mentally there. His legs are not broken. His burns will heal and none of them are that deep that the agony will go on for too long. But no matter how much I try to sugarcoat it, this whole situation and how lucky I feel to still have him with me. His recovery is going to be long and arduous. How I'm going to manage it, I have no idea.

I buy a pack of plain chocolate M&Ms and promise myself to only have a couple. A few minutes later, the bag is gone. It's a compulsive thing to just eat when stressed, uncertain, and bored. No matter how many times I've tried to do any of those intentional eating diets or anything like that, I've become convinced that that kind of stuff only works for people who don't have stressful lives.

I'm angry with Keith Folger. I am pissed that he was using drugs and put Dylan in this situation. But he's dead and there's only so much anger that can be sent his way.

The truth is that I completely sympathize and understand. I've never tried hard drugs. Even a few puffs of marijuana made me sick to my stomach because I have a low tolerance, and sugar has always done the trick.

But I also sympathize. When you're not in control of your life, you tend to turn to your vices to deal with everything as best as you can.

Leaning against the wall and kicking my shoe against the linoleum floor, I debate as to whether or not to get a Snickers bar. An older man with salt and pepper hair, and incredibly kind eyes, approaches me.

"Excuse me, ma'am. Are you Charlotte Pierce?"

"Yes," I say, crumbling the M&M pack in my left hand to hide the evidence for some reason.

"I just want to introduce myself. I'm Dylan's father, Deacon Ferreira. The nurse said that you were around and we just wanted to meet you. Dylan has told me so much about you."

"Oh, wow. Yes, of course. I'm sorry. I was just going to come over to chat, but I got quite famished."

At that moment, a wrapper falls to the floor and I'm embarrassed that this is what I have turned to, to quench my hunger.

"Plain M&Ms. They're a favorite of mine, too."

He smiles and gives me a wink. There's something about him that's so relaxing. Perhaps it's his voice, but it's not just that. It's his demeanor, too.

"Did you get a chance to see Dylan?"

"Yes," I say. "How about you?"

"Earlier this morning. They called us and we took the first flight down."

"Oh, that's great. I'm glad that you got to see him. He's doing quite well considering, don't you think, Deacon?" I say.

"Hopefully."

"Yes. I was really scared that it would be much worse. I guess the recovery's going to take months, but he should be out of the hospital much sooner than that."

"Yes. When they first called," Deacon shakes his head, "we just weren't sure what was going to happen and it was one stressful flight. Let's just say that I ate about five of those."

"You're a man after my own heart," I say with a smile. "I like that you assess your stress level by the amount of candy you consume."

"Well, it's as good of a metric as anything else, isn't it?"

He smiles and I smile, too. Despite the odds, despite what's happened to his son, his attitude is positive and lighthearted, and I'm immediately drawn to him and how he is in the world.

He reminds me of the way that teachers are sometimes portrayed in movies where they uplift a community of kids that were forgotten. He's somebody who sees someone in you, someone who believes that everything will be okay, despite all the odds. I've never had a teacher like that. Hardly anyone memorable at all, but I always wanted to believe in me like that.

Deacon asks if I would like to sit down in the waiting room and have some coffee with him. It's his treat and he buys two cups from the vending machine. We both find it rather gross and I offer to make up for it by going to Starbucks in town.

"Dylan has told us a lot about you," Deacon says. "You used to work for the LAPD and now down in Palm Valley, what brought you over there?"

I shrug. "Wanted to get away from the hustle and bustle of a big city department. It was very stressful, lots of politics as well, and it wasn't really my jam. I did a lateral move and luckily they had an opening. Palm Valley isn't exactly a small town, it's a suburban city, but the county itself is quite rural as you know. Occasionally, there are cases that are a little bit different."

"Like what?" he asks.

"Well, like the one that we're currently working on. It's macabre so I don't want to tell you about it if you want to think about something positive and happy."

"Oh, no, I'd love to hear what you're working on. I'm a writer, so I'm always curious about that stuff."

"Oh, yes, of course. Dylan told me that you're a big-time author working on a book on JFK."

"More like procrastinating, but I teach a number of classes and I love to hear stories. Stories are the lifeblood of my life."

For some reason, despite the fact that I have only just met him, I want to share. I don't go into too many details about the two boys, but enough to paint a picture. He's clearly interested.

"This is an unusual case," I say. "Most of my investigations are much more mundane. So much from getting away from the city, huh?"

"Well, at least there's not that much gang activity and general crime, even if a serial killer seems to be hunting," he jokes.

"Thanks." I smile, enjoying the banter.

"That's where you were leading me to, right? That somebody's out there taking little boys?"

"Yes, unfortunately, that seems to be what's happening."

"Well, I wish you all the best on the case," Deacon says. "And I'd love to know who did it after you solve it."

"Ah, *if* we solve it." I correct him.

He looks surprised.

"You know the rule about solving the murder in the first forty-eight hours? That's not just TV schtick. That's true. The longer they go on, the less likely they'll be solved and now we're talking about two cases in the same county, but separated by distance. I have no idea if they're related. I mean, likely yes, but I have no real proof except for the casings are the same and they disappeared and were killed under similar circumstances. I just hope that no one else is taken."

24

CHARLOTTE

Just at that moment, a woman dressed in a comfortable but elegant outfit comes out from Dylan's room. She looks to be about the same age as Deacon. And he gives her a quick peck on the cheek when she approaches him. He introduces us and Mara sits down in the seat next to her husband, looking at me with the same wide-eyed expression.

"How's Dylan doing?" I ask.

"Really well considering. You saw him, right?" I nod.

"His spirits are up. He's so happy that we're all here, but he's clearly in pain. He's going to take a nap now because when they up the medication it usually makes him fall asleep."

Mara gives me a few updates which are not really any new information but I'm glad to hear that he's doing well. We're all very thankful that this wasn't worse and his fate didn't follow Folger's. I don't know whether or not I'm allowed to share about his use of methamphetamines. I decide to keep it to myself for now.

"Being a firefighter is dangerous," Deacon says.

"Probably not any more so than a cop," Mara pipes in.

She's referring to Dylan's oldest brother, the one he doesn't mention much.

"I just wish that he had pursued something in finance or private equity, too. Remember he had all those offers, he even worked for a year."

"Yes, but he wasn't that into it. What can we do about it now, Mara? Our son fights wildfires which are a major problem in California and are just going to get worse. He was taking all precautions. Somebody has to do it," Deacon says.

"But why does it have to be our son? That's not fair."

"You know you're not being fair to him."

"No," Mara says. "He wasn't. He was enjoying his job more than being a detective in San Francisco, but that's not saying much. You know what had happened. You know why he left when his partner got killed, and now look, somebody gets killed again."

"Well, look at the bright side, maybe he'll leave now."

"Don't be funny."

Even though they're bickering back and forth, there's nothing malicious about it. They don't seem angry with each other, just sad and tired. I want to tell them that there's nothing wrong with being a firefighter, but my statement would be disproved right now, right at this moment, given what has just happened. It is a dangerous job, especially wildfires, they're unpredictable. The wind can change directions at any moment and surround you and sometimes the people that are supposed to be watching your back aren't doing that at all.

Dylan's parents probably don't know how much I know about him and continue their conversation in a hushed tone. Going through history, they talk about him becoming a cop to find John, his missing brother, and then quitting when his partner got ambushed and killed. They think that what drove him to become a firefighter was meaningful work that's a lot less political than being a cop, but it's nevertheless quite dangerous.

You might not be dealing with dangerous criminals, but nature can be just as deadly and unpredictable.

A little bit later, Mara turns her attention to me. Unlike her husband, she's anxious and nervous but nevertheless pleasant and polite. We chat for a little while about nothing in particular and when she and Deacon start to bicker again, I see an opportunity to escape and tell them that I have to make some calls.

This is the last place that I thought I would meet my boyfriend's parents, in the waiting room right outside his door while he lays there with second and third degree burns.

PRIOR TO GOING to town to grab some dinner, I pop by the waiting room to ask if Deacon and Mara want anything. But they want to go by themselves. I get it. They want to get out of here to clear their heads.

Dylan is still asleep. Just as I'm about to leave, I spot a nurse on the way to his room with an enormous bouquet of flowers. She drops the card and when I pick it up, I spot the name at the bottom. Kelsey Hall.

Kelsey sent him flowers? How would she even know about this? I wonder. Then I remember that one of the calls that I made on my way up to the hospital was to her. It had gone to voice mail, but I had mentioned that I was going to see my boyfriend who was in an accident.

Kelsey answers on the second ring.

"Thank you so much for the flowers. You really didn't have to send anything," I say into the phone propped up on my dash. I drive down the narrow winding streets through the pines, heading to town.

"Well, you said he was hurt, it's the least I can do. How's he doing?"

I fill her in and thank her again for thinking of him.

We stay on the line a little bit and for a moment, I'm uncertain as to what to say. This is a friend who I haven't talked to seriously in years and it feels both odd and familiar.

"I'm sorry, I haven't had a chance to work on your case much. These murders here have been occupying all of my time, and then this happened with Dylan."

"No, it's fine," Kelsey says. "It's nice to hear your voice."

"I've missed you, too," I admit.

"I know that you promised to call when you found something, but would you be okay to just talk sometimes, outside of that? Like friends do?"

"Of course. I'd like that," I say.

I consider pulling into the drive-through and decide against it. Instead, I stay on the line and ask her about her day and her kids.

"I have a PTA teacher appreciation thing coming up this week, so we're planning a big dinner for the teacher who is retiring."

"That sounds fun."

"It is actually. It's normal and I like that. But stressful, too."

"What else have you been up to?" I ask after a brief pause.

"Went to the gym today after a really long time off. It felt good. I really need to make it a habit."

Kelsey's doing her best to make this conversation as normal as possible and I appreciate that. It's distracting, in a good way.

"I can't remember the last time I was at the gym," I admit. "All I did today is stress eat, unfortunately. I ate a pack of M&Ms and it took all of my strength not to eat three others."

"Oh, I get it," she says, and by the tone of her voice, I can tell that she's smiling. "Maybe we can be like each other's accountability partners. I mean, I know we're living apart, but maybe we can keep each other on track with workouts, food, that kind of thing."

"Huh, I'd like that," I say. "I've never done that with anyone before."

"What's your goal in terms of going to the gym? I mean, not right now, but in general?" she asks.

"I would say five days a week would be ideal, but it'd be great if it was three."

"Good. Well, why don't you aim for three? If you don't go to the gym, just get some exercise, maybe a certain number of steps or something like that."

"Okay, I have my Apple watch. I wear it every day, but have been too scared to check the step count," I admit, only half-jokingly.

"I know what you mean. I haven't stepped on the scale in about two months and every day that passes, it just builds in anticipation."

"You should just do it," I say, giving her advice that I want to take myself.

"Just go ahead and don't beat yourself up no matter what it is. Do it so you'll have a baseline. I'm saying that like I do it every day. Of course, I don't," I say, shaking my head. "But that would be the advice that I would give you and this other version of me that would listen to my own advice."

We laugh and chuckle, and it feels so good to have a friend to talk to. We chat for about ten more minutes before ending on a high note. She asks me to text her any updates about Dylan because she wants to know. I promise that I will because I want to share.

After having dinner and a Grande iced coffee at Starbucks, I return back to the hospital to see Dylan.

25

CHARLOTTE

I spend the night in a comfortable motel room that has curtains with little bears on them and bright green shaggy carpet. Dylan slept all evening and I came here late at night, falling asleep quickly under the well-worn blush-colored bedspread.

When I visit Dylan the following morning, he's in better spirits and using a lot less medication than before. We chat, play games on the iPad, and watch a show, trying to be as normal as possible.

When his parents stop by with breakfast, we all try to think of something to talk about that isn't *this*. I want to know more about the recovery rehab, when he can be discharged, and every other detail. But bringing that up puts a damper on the afternoon. Instead, we play a game of Uno and it's nice to have something else to think about.

Around lunch, I suddenly remember that I have dinner plans with my father, and I haven't told him anything about this yet. I go to the waiting room to give him a call, hiding in the corner and keeping my voice low so as not to bother the other visitors.

After I say a brief hello, I fill him in on what happened with Dylan and tell him that I have to cancel dinner tonight.

"You can't make the drive down?"

"Well, I'm two hours away, and I'm staying here for a few days using my time off because he's seriously injured."

"I'm really sorry that this has happened to your friend, but I don't see how it's going to interfere with our plans," Dad says.

I can hear the smugness in his voice.

"He has to stay in the hospital and then he's going to need a lot of help to get back on his feet," I continue to explain myself, feeling like I'm a teenager asking permission.

"That's my point exactly, Charlotte. We have plans to have dinner. He's still going to be in the hospital for days to come, and the recovery's going to take a long time. He's fine where he is. I don't see why you can't be bothered to keep one basic commitment."

I scoff into the phone shaking my head.

"You know that I'm not in Southern California that often, I'm going out of my way to drive to see you because of *your* work schedule."

"*My* work schedule?" I snap, raising my voice a little bit. "You know, you're not doing me any favors. I don't need this. I thought we were spending time together to enjoy each other's company. I don't find this that enjoyable."

"Charlotte-" Dad starts to say something, but I cut him off.

"If you don't want to see me on my terms, you don't have to. I made that perfectly clear all of those years ago."

"I'm your father, Charlotte."

"Yes, I know and as my father, I thought you would understand that my *boyfriend*, not just my friend, was almost killed fighting wildfires. I want to stay here at the hospital and be with him, lift his spirits, show him that I'm thinking of him. I know that you have taken the time to drive out to Palm Valley. That's why

I called earlier, to tell you that you don't have to do that. Just stay in LA, however long you need to for work and then go home."

There's a long pause on the other end, as he tries to figure out what to say, but I guess he can't, so I wait. I'm tempted to hang up, but instead I just give him space.

"Can I expect you in DC, the weekend of my lifetime achievement award?" Dad asks.

"I don't know," I say, trying to remember when that will even be.

"Your stepmother is putting it all together. I expect you to be there. If you don't do it for me, do it for her and for this family," he says and hangs up.

What a great relationship I have with my father, I think to myself.

A teen girl, no older than fifteen looks up at me from one of the waiting room chairs. Her legs are tucked in under her, her arms wrapped around her knees.

"That was my dad," I explain, rolling my eyes. "It has been like that since I was your age."

She nods and smiles as if she knows what I'm dealing with all too well. The self-centeredness is difficult to describe to people who don't have parents like this.

I see Dylan with his parents and how they have dropped everything to be here for him. Even if they didn't need to come. Even if he's okay, it's nice that they are keeping him company.

They are friends. Real friends. Maybe they don't tell him what to do anymore. Perhaps they shouldn't. In fact, their relationship is probably better for it.

My father, on the other hand, oscillates between treating me like a two-year-old and an eight-year-old. On the surface, he knows that I'm capable of a lot, that I'm an adult but he also expects me to structure my whole life around him. This hasn't been possible in years, and it hasn't been something I wanted for much longer than that.

I don't want to go to his lifetime achievement award dinner, celebrate him and his valiant career but maybe I should. His career is the one thing in his life that he did right. It's also the reason why he messed up all the other parts of it.

Also, Sherry will be there, and so will my siblings who I haven't seen in far too long. Maybe if Dylan is feeling better, he can come as well and I won't be the only single one there. But as far as these dinners go, I don't know if I'm going to keep that up after this. It's just too much of a commitment, and I don't want to give him the opportunity to make me feel crappy about myself, which happens at most of these dinners anyway.

Every time he says, "You would have made a great FBI agent," I can hear the regret in his voice. It's supposed to be a compliment but it's anything but that. He's telling me that I messed up. He's saying that the choices I made were no good, and if he had had more control, he would have made better ones.

When I see Dylan's parents head down the hallway, I wave hello and then turn around and walk the other direction. I'm too angry and pissed off to talk to them now. Instead, I head out into the woods behind the hospital.

The sky is impossibly blue. The towering trees with trunks the color of burnt orange sway in the slight breeze. I inhale the scent of pine needles roasting in the summer heat.

I take one breath after another. Walking further and further up the hill, I leave the trail and head into the unknown. The trees are far enough apart that you can see where you're going and a few hundred feet off the road, nature explodes in all of her glory on this beautiful summer day. Squirrels hop on branches. Lizards sunbathe on rocks. Birds sing their hearts out.

The higher I go up the mountain, the sweatier yesterday's t-shirt and jeans get. I give myself a sniff shaking my head, regretting not stopping by a pharmacy to get some deodorant. I add that to my mental to-do list in addition to the eyeliner, foundation, and mascara. You'd be surprised how even a little smidge of it keeps those comments about looking tired and questions about sleeping away.

Taking out my phone, I text Kelsey about what happened with my dad. I guess I could call, but I think that would just send my blood boiling even more. So, I summarize the story instead and send her a lengthy post. She writes back almost immediately.

God, I'm so sorry. That really sucks. He hasn't changed much, has he?

I remember that she knew him only as a child and how he used to force me to work out every day. It was his way of keeping me in shape but mostly to just control me.

Not really. I don't see him much now except for these dinners and I actually did not expect him to get so mad about me canceling. I still don't quite understand why he did. I at least saved him a trip all the way from LA to Palm Valley.

We text back and forth and it gives me space to write back if I want to, and collect my thoughts if I need to.

I stay in the forest for another hour enjoying nature. My texts with Kelsey move on from my dad to her kids to the weather. After a little while, it's like we're real friends again. Just keeping in touch throughout the day for no reason whatsoever, providing little updates of life to one another.

When I get back to the hospital room, Dylan is taking a nap again. I spend time with his parents talking about writing and literature and books. They seem more relaxed today. Reserved, not so worried like they were before. It's that point where you've accepted what has happened and are now just trying to put the pieces together of how to move forward. Luckily, with time, the burns will heal and he should be as good as new except for the possible scar tissue.

Dylan's dad puts me so much at ease and I ask him about everything that he has written and his career, in general. Just as I'm about to open up to him about my own attempts at writing, my phone rings.

"I'm sorry, I have to take this. It's my partner," I say, excusing myself.

"Hey, sorry for calling you, but something serious has happened," Will says.

I hold my breath.

"Another kid was taken," Will says. "He was biking outside his house when he disappeared. We haven't found a body. Not yet anyway. There's a chance that he might still be alive, but the killer is probably one and the same. You really have to get back here."

26

CHARLOTTE

I head back home a few minutes after I receive the call from Will. The case is breaking and I need to be there to help them figure out who did this. Dylan's parents understand and promise to tell me when he's awake so I can call him and explain. Part of the reason that I'm leaving is that he is better, and everything is taken care of, and now all he needs to heal is time. Part of it is that I know that Philip is a scumbag who will mess up this case to get to me, and those parents of the murdered victims and the missing one deserve to know the truth. If I can do anything to help, I must.

Will texted me the address of the apartment complex where this happened and I find him sitting in his car, playing on his phone. My knock startles him.

"Thanks for coming," he says. "Otherwise, they would have stuck me with that FBI agent."

I clench my jaw and give him a nod.

"How's Dylan doing?"

I update him a little bit, but I can tell that he's not really listening.

"Tell me what happened with this kid."

Will looks worn out, his shirt is untucked and wrinkled, not exactly screaming professionalism. When I point to it, he tucks it in promptly and gives me a nod as a thank you.

"What happened? Why do you look so wrecked?" I ask.

"Didn't get much sleep last night. I wasn't supposed to be working today. We went out and I had a little bit too much to drink."

"That sucks, I'm sorry."

"I'm sorry to get you involved. You weren't partying, you were in the hospital with your boyfriend, and you're still here."

"Thanks for calling. I want to get this sadistic ass as much as you do. We can't let him wander the streets without any consequences."

"I'm getting so tired of hearing the same story over and over," he admits, looking broken. "What if we can't find him?"

"We can and we will," I promise. "He's going to make a mistake. He's going to leave a trace somewhere, and that's when we're going to pounce."

"I really hope so."

"Tell me about this case," I say.

"I talked to the parents earlier. They are really shook up. That's why I wanted you to be here for the second interview. They're still searching for him. They seem so lost and I get it. I haven't tied it to the other two cases yet but it's very similar."

I curse under my breath and follow him to the double-decker apartment building.

"This is unusual, isn't it?" I ask.

"The other kids did go missing in rural areas," Will says. "That could be significant or not. He could be more of an opportunist."

THE SIGN OUT front of the two-story building has a sign that says, *Now Leasing*. It goes about half a block with about thirty units in total. The front is lined with carports, surrounded by shrubs and a bit of landscaping to make it look a bit nicer. It's definitely not a new building but it's well taken care of and loved.

It looks nice, a place that you would let your kid ride his bike outside. I wonder how many residents were home at the time when this happened. The parents noticed that he was gone around nine in the morning. Most people were probably at work, but I hope there's a nosy grandma or two who liked looking out of the window. We can only hope. The deputies canvassed and interviewed a few of them. We have the reports, but we definitely have to do a more thorough search.

Will and I head upstairs, make our way across the catwalk, and knock on apartment number fifteen, at the far end. There's no enclosed foyer or anything like that and the door opens directly into the living room. This isn't exactly uncommon in a warm desert climate where there's no snow and little rain to contend with most of the year. The need for hallways and places to get mud off your shoes isn't exactly necessary.

After one knock, Mrs. Gomez answers the door and immediately calls for Ricardo, her husband. They both speak perfect English without a tinge of an accent and invite us inside with tears in their eyes.

The apartment is a spacious three bedroom probably around fifteen hundred square feet. It has recently been remodeled with shaker-style kitchen cabinets and new vinyl flooring.

The Gomezes keep it immaculate, modern and upscale. The walls are adorned with mirrors and artwork, some of which look like it belongs to the little boy.

We sit on their mid-century modern sofa and Mrs. Gomez offers us something to drink and eat, but we decline.

I pull out my notepad and so does Will. I sometimes use these as a crutch to not meet their eyes when they are particularly overcome with emotion.

Child abduction cases are the hardest. You want to give the parents hope, solace, and support, but we weren't exactly taught any of that at the academy. Whatever support I offer is completely self-taught, most of it is advice from therapists on YouTube.

It's really when I see their pain that it becomes the hardest for me. My empathy meter goes through the roof and I want to reach out and give them a hug, but I'm afraid that I'll break down myself. That happened to me once, much to my own embarrassment.

I'd had three years on the job and I'd started to be a lot less cautious of my own feelings. I thought I could handle it. I thought I could handle everything. Then I met a mother who was crying for her teenage daughter who went missing. We found her, murdered, her body dumped in the garbage behind their building.

When I did a follow-up interview to ask the mother for more details, she broke down again. For some reason, I reached over to touch her hand, and when our fingers collided, I just felt this rush of emotion go through me and I began to cry. It was highly unprofessional and it would have made me the mockery of the department. Luckily, it wasn't on tape or on camera, but at her home. I apologized profusely for that, but she later told me that she appreciated that so much because it felt like I cared. Perhaps it's not a weakness after all, despite what the department would have you believe.

Nevertheless, I haven't broken down since. Keeping everything bottled up and focusing on note-taking has been a blessing in that regard. It takes me out of the moment. I can be someone who records what's going on, a casual observer, rather than the person who is actually living through this.

Mrs. Gomez cries quietly into her hands as Will asks questions. It's a repeat of what I know they have gone through before.

27

CHARLOTTE

Ari was riding his bike at around nine in the morning. He's six years old, has dark curly hair, olive skin, and loves mostly animals and garbage trucks.

I pay attention to what the parents say while Will talks to them. I notice that not once do they use the past tense. I'm also well aware of the fact that they know that in a couple of hours, it's going to become evening, and then in a couple more, it's going to be night.

They're worried about their little boy spending a night alone out there in the elements.

"I just have no idea what could have happened. He always stays right in the parking lot," Mr. Gomez says.

"When did you notice that he was missing?" I ask.

"He'll usually ride his bike around for twenty, thirty minutes and then come back, have some water, play with some toys, that kind of thing, but he didn't this time."

"Why wasn't he at school?" I ask. "Shouldn't he be in kindergarten, preschool?"

"He actually attends a preschool," Mrs. Gomez says. "But he's had this cough for a while now and he had a runny nose. We decided to keep him home, so he doesn't get anyone else sick. But after a couple of hours of sitting on the couch, he got bored and said he wanted to ride his bike. You can't stop kids sometimes from being kids."

"Uh-huh." I nod.

"I figured he'd get worn out in maybe fifteen minutes, and if I stand right here looking out this window, I can see him. I did for a bit, but then, I remembered that I had to do some meal prep and it would probably be a good time to do that now rather than when he was back, distracting me, talking to me, and asking me for things. You know how kids are."

She nods at me expecting me to commiserate, and I do.

"When was the first time that you noticed that he wasn't there?" I ask.

"About forty minutes later, I realized that it had been a while. I just glanced out the window and I didn't see him, but it's not unusual. I went out on the landing to look closer. I yelled his name, and he wasn't there."

Her voice cracks at that moment. Her eyes dart from side to side, looking to me for help.

"I should have gone out there sooner. I shouldn't have done all that stupid meal prepping. It's just.... I can't believe how irresponsible I was."

Her husband drapes his arm over her shoulder as she sobs.

"It's not your fault, Cecilia. We're going to find him," he says.

She puts her head on his shoulder and lets out a deep breath.

"That's when you called the police?" I ask.

"I ran out. I looked around for him everywhere. I knew that he wouldn't leave the parking lot because we told him not to and he always listened to what we said. Then I saw his bike in that irrigation ditch right over there. It's a little bit out of sight. It was thrown there as if like, you weren't supposed to see it, and I knew that something terrible had happened. That's when I called."

"Can you tell us anything that's going on?" Mr. Gomez asks.

"The deputies have interviewed a number of the neighbors and we're going to be talking to people across the street as well," Will says. "We're going to be collecting data from cameras and even cameras that may be inside vehicles. We're very hopeful that we will find something that will lead us to some answers."

It seems to help them somewhat, but I can tell that they're not fully satisfied. I know that Will had mentioned that they don't know about the other missing kids, and I wonder if it's best to bring it up or keep them in the dark.

It's not that I want them to hold on to false hope. It's that I don't want to make them believe that something worse has happened to their son than they already think. I don't want to give them any confirmation of this horrible thing that might have happened.

I decide it's best to give Will leeway in the decision as to whether to say something or not and he doesn't.

We offer our condolences, and we promise to do as much as we can. Finally, leaving the interview with heavy hearts, we walk over to the irrigation ditch and Will shows me where the bike was found. You can't really see it from the street, but it's right outside where the carports start.

"Whoever did this drove in, grabbed the boy, hid the bike, and then drove out," Will says. "I just hope that there are cameras here. I mean there're so many people, maybe someone has something."

Without further ado, we begin. We start knocking on doors, asking questions. This is the cop's real job. The feet on the pavement method of uncovering who committed the crime. In movies and TV shows, this part of the job is rarely shown, maybe a couple of interviews here and there.

In reality, it takes almost the entire day of speaking to everyone, reviewing the stories, telling them a little bit about what happened, giving them our condolences if they knew the child. There's a lot of emotional labor that goes into this job. By the time the day is coming to an end, I feel spent and so exhausted that I could sleep for maybe twenty hours.

I have high hopes but little expectation that the people in this building have a lot of cameras. I am pleasantly surprised by the sheer amount of footage we get.

You'd be surprised by how many people in gated communities with guards have armed response security and Nest cameras all over their houses from all different angles, and how many people who live in places that are more likely to have crime have none of those protections. Cameras, of course, are more of a deterrent than anything else, especially visible ones, but they do require an initial investment, and they can, of course, be stolen.

When we get back to the station and review the footage that we collected, one thing stands out. One of the neighbors, an older man in apartment thirteen has had his car vandalized, and so he set up a camera right outside his carport, catching video of little Ari going back and forth on his bicycle. The last sighting is around 9:20, nothing else after. On the camera set up by the young woman in her twenties focused on her car from the other angle, shows a motorcycle, a black Harley, pull in front of the apartment building.

It goes slightly out of view for a little while, one minute and fifty-seven seconds exactly, and then he steps on the accelerator and rushes out with something or someone in front of him. We zoom in and go through the footage over and over again. It looks like either a giant package or a small boy.

"That has to be him," I say.

Will is less convinced, but he agrees that this is the best lead we have. Luckily, we also have part of the license plate when the motorcycle turns around the corner.

"This is it," I say. "We have to search for this number."

Even though we're both dog-tired, we put the license plate into the search and come up with the name, Keith Moraine, forty-four years old with a mustache and blue eyes. He has no record, at least not in California, and we need the FBI database for more than that.

"We have to put an APB out on this guy," I say. "He has to be the one who took him."

"Yes, for sure."

We call the lieutenant at home, explain what we found, and get everything arranged. Now the name of the game is waiting. The license plate and the name are going to go into the system, and deputies all over California are going to be notified to be on the lookout for this guy.

I argue for the fact that we should put out an Amber Alert for him. This is an alert that tells law enforcement agencies that a child has been taken by this man and gives some extra notification and urgency to the matter. But the lieutenant says there isn't enough evidence, that Amber Alerts are usually done with witness information, not a video that isn't particularly clear. An APB would have to do for now as that's all we have.

"I'm going to catch up on some work here," Will says just as I'm about to grab my bag and head home.

"You have to get some sleep. It's been a long day," I say. "I know you're just going to wait to see if an APB picks up the bike, aren't you?"

He nods.

"You're just going to exhaust yourself. The chances of someone finding him in the next couple of hours are slim and you can just go home and relax in the meantime. They'll call us for sure."

"Yes, I know." He nods. "I just can't relax."

"You want to go get a drink?" I ask. "We're technically off."

"Yes, but what if they call, then we'll be back on duty."

"I know, but it'd be something."

We talk about it, debate the pros and cons, and decide that the best thing to do is to just go home, fall into bed, and get some sleep.

"I'm sure Erin is waiting for you. How's her pregnancy going?"

"She's sick all the time, throwing up a lot. I wish she would just eat everything in sight."

"She would probably prefer that, too, but you have to be there for her. Help her out, hold her hair back."

"I'm trying."

"Will, I'm serious. She needs your help. I know that you can be quite helpful at work, but in your personal relationships, you can be quite distant."

"How would you know anything about it?" he snaps.

"Well, let's see. You are a thirty-six-year-old man, who's only now getting into a serious relationship for the first time ever with a girl that you used to date."

"She's the one who got away," Will says, smacking his lips. "I was just waiting for her the whole time."

"Okay, that's really fucking sweet, saccharin, and almost disgusting. Why don't you just go home and say that to Erin, who will appreciate that kind of sentiment?"

I smile at him and he smiles back, and for a moment, we forget all about this horrible day and just try to make the best of things. Will walks me out to the car.

"Take care, okay? Let me know if that Philip guy shows up and causes any trouble."

"I will," I say.

"I'm serious, Charlotte. He's really messed up and I'm worried about you being back here."

"I'm going to be fine. I'm armed, right? Armed and dangerous." I smile, half-joking, but knowing full well that he's completely right about worrying about Philip.

28

CHARLOTTE

The following morning at breakfast, I sit down with my phone, stare into the black abyss of my coffee cup, and wonder how it is that I got almost eight hours of sleep, but very little rest.

I haven't talked to Dylan yet. I'm just about to call.

It's in those few hours, a few minutes of reverie where you're just alone with your thoughts, that everything comes back to you.

The new case has a to-do list, the length of the Amazon River.

Frankly, I'm not sure if we'll be able to get most of it done as quickly as we should.

Other deputies can help, of course, and they will, but I'm a bit of a control freak.

The thing about letting other people do the interviews and talking to all the witnesses is that if they don't do it exactly right, they may not notice that something is off when it is, and there's no way that I would ever be able to catch it again.

There's something to that first interview, that first contact with a potential witness that sets the tone and the mood for everything else.

If it isn't right, it's hard to recover.

As far as relying on their instincts, as much as I would love to, it's hard at this point.

They're deputies. They mean well, but it might be mistakes are made just because they don't have the proper investigative training.

To try to stop this train of thought from consuming my morning, I jump on the treadmill, put it at 2.5 miles per hour, and just walk.

I haven't run in a while, but even the little bit of exercise is better than nothing.

I put the iPad in front of me, scroll through YouTube, find a few funny reaction videos, and let them roll, taking my thoughts elsewhere.

I turn up the incline, climb all the way to seven, and walk on three.

I could break out into a run or a jog, but it's nice to just space out, not think about much.

If I'm struggling to breathe on a run, it tends to take me out of everything.

"Hey there," someone says, startling me.

I look up to see that it's Agent Philip Welch leaning casually on the wall like he had been there for some time.

"What are you doing here?"

I pull my AirPods out of my ears and struggle to turn down the speed at which I'm walking.

"Your door was open. I came to talk to you, I didn't have your number."

"So, you just showed up? I'm going to be at the office."

"Yes, but this is more of a private conversation," he says with a little bit of a smirk.

His suit fits perfectly.

His cuticles are manicured.

His hair is slicked back.

He's put together rather nicely, almost like he's going in for a job interview.

Is this all meant to impress me?

I have no idea. Maybe it's just some sort of egomaniacal trip that he's on and has been on for years.

I hate the fact that he is in my primary bedroom, standing there, looking all around at the pictures on the walls, the long sleeve shirt that I was wearing earlier in the day that I had tossed onto the half-made bed.

I try to act like it's all normal.

I take a deep breath, walking past him.

He reaches over to touch my arm, but luckily, the hallway is just wide enough for me to avoid his fingers.

I lead him to the kitchen, holding my phone, turned on, ready to do what exactly? Call 911?

I'm a freaking cop, a detective, but I know full well that my on-duty weapon is in the locker at the station and my off-duty one is in pieces on my vanity, I had just cleaned it, didn't put it back together yet.

I'm sure that he knows that given that he walked past the primary bathroom on the way here.

"How are you doing, Charlotte?" Philip asks, leaning against the wall.

Everything about him is condescending, full of jest.

His confidence is disgusting, but there's nothing I can do to change any of that.

Most people in his position would be scared that I would talk, that I would come forward and say something to someone, but he's not.

He's still certain that he'll never be caught. He's taunting me, which makes me feel like crap.

"What are you doing here?" I ask him point-blank, heading toward the kitchen. "Why did you just break into my house? To talk to me about what exactly?"

"I didn't break into your house. The door was open."

"I lock my doors every day, and I know that for sure."

"You can go look."

I glance back. "Whatever lock breaking device you used, that's not going to convince me that my door was open. I know you better than that."

"Well, I just wanted to stop by and talk to you about the case," Philip says as if this is the most normal thing in the world. "I miss you."

"Do you want to talk about the case or do you miss me?" I challenge him. He shrugs.

"Listen, I'll work with you on this case. That's fine, but we're not going to be friends or anything beyond that."

"Come on, please, Charlotte. I don't want to start off on a bad foot."

"You mean like when you sexually assaulted me?"

"I did no such thing. You were totally into it. You just don't remember because you drank too much."

"You keep telling yourself that story." I nod. "You and I both know the truth though."

"Why don't you give me another chance?"

"You're all out of chances," I say. "I need you to get out of my house. Do you want to discuss the case? Do you have anything constructive to say to me?"

"Yes."

"Okay, then we can do so at the office."

"I thought we could keep it more casual," he insists.

I shake my head no. "That's the last thing I want. That's the last thing I need."

He takes a step closer to me. My heart starts to beat in my chest. I look around but I had not positioned myself anywhere near the knives. How stupid. They're all the way across the kitchen behind him.

I make my hand into a fist. He looks at it.

"What are you going to do? Punch me?" he asks.

My other hand is behind me. I'm holding my phone, and I wish that I could feel the buttons so that I can open it. Unfortunately, I haven't had a blackberry in years. I know that it won't let me in without a face ID.

Philip takes a step closer to me. I pull away and turn toward the pantry. The door is slightly ajar. I walk in.

"Where are you going?"

I close the door in his face, flip on the light, and turn on my phone. When he opens the door back up, I'm holding a pack of chips.

"Just got hungry," I say.

Philip gives me space to walk past him.

"Do you really eat chips for breakfast?"

"Look, whatever I do or don't do is none of your concern. Why don't you just mind your own business?"

"Tell me about the third missing boy. How likely do you think it is that his murder is related to the first two?" he asks.

"Well, first of all, we have no idea if it's a murder," I correct him.

"Not yet. The other two bodies were found right nearby. This one, it's yet to be located."

"What about everything else? It's a match, isn't it?"

"It is," I agree.

"It's something to consider."

"I'm not sure, what do you think?"

"Oh, are you asking my professional opinion now?" Philip asks.

"Why not? You're here. You're an FBI agent."

I tilt my head to one side.

"We just have two kids missing from their bikes murdered right away. This one's missing. Maybe he was taken somewhere, but it could be a totally unrelated case."

"Basically you're saying that we have no idea." I sum up his position. He shrugs. "Good. Just thought that I was mistaken."

"I don't know why you have to make everything so difficult, Charlotte."

He takes another step toward me. I walk backward until my butt is against the counter. One quick movement and I pull a knife out of the block, but when I turn to face him, he presses a blade to my neck.

"You don't think I'm watching you, Charlotte? You don't think I know what you're up to?"

"What am I up to?" I say, holding onto my knife blade, breathing deeply against it.

"I just don't know why you have to make this so difficult. Why won't you be my friend?"

"You're threatening me and you're asking me why I won't be your friend?" I ask. "How about this? I went on a date with you, you drugged me, and you assaulted me. Raped me probably. I got a rape kit done, but I was stupid and didn't get it submitted."

"You got a rape kit done?" he asks.

"Yes, why, are you worried about that?" I ask.

"No, I just didn't realize you went that far."

"So you're admitting the fact that I didn't just make it all up. That you were there?"

"Hey, I'm not admitting anything. I'm just surprised. How come the cops didn't come after me?" he asks.

"You know why."

"Oh, yes, because no one would believe you."

"Because I was a rookie cop. Because I was an idiot and a girl, that's why. Because I wanted to just forget it because you humiliated me so much, but now I realize that I should have made you pay because you won't understand anything until you know what it feels like to get abused like that."

That statement stresses him. A big vein in his forehead starts to pump as he clenches his jaw.

"We were just having fun, Charlotte. I don't know why you have to take it so seriously."

"I think anyone being assaulted is quite a serious matter."

"Well, I don't," he says.

"Why? Because you do it all the time?"

He shrugs and gives me a wink.

"Fine. You want me to leave? I'll leave," Philip says, putting the knife down. "But don't you ever threaten me. I'll come after you and I'll do much worse than what I did before. No one is going to believe *you* that I would do anything like that because I work for the FBI."

Now it's my turn to clench my jaw. I wait for him to leave and watch him go through the door. I let out a sigh of relief and look down at my hand.

The phone is still on, the recording still going.

"He said that, he really said that," I whisper out loud and see the squiggly line go up and down on the screen, recording my words.

I let out a sigh of relief. Without waiting a moment longer, I press Save.

Scrolling feverishly, I type in my email address and then Will's and Dylan's. They are the people I trust most in the world.

Suddenly, the door swings open and Philip rushes at me.

I reach for the send button, but he grabs the phone out of my hand before I can do it.

He's holding a gun, pointing it at me.

"Yes, that's what I thought happened. I wondered why you had to go into that pantry. Suddenly had this insatiable need for chips?" He shakes his head and a smile washes over his face. "You needed to go in there to access your phone, turn it on. Did you get a recording of all of this? You think that's going to be your proof?"

Philip turns the screen toward me. It scans my face. The first thing that pops up is, unfortunately, the recording itself. He scrolls back, listens to a few bars of it. Shaking his head, I see him press Delete.

I swallow hard, realizing that I hadn't had a chance to email it to anyone yet.

I consider throwing myself at him trying to grab the phone, but I'm worried that he'll just shoot me and kill me right here.

Getting proof isn't worth that.

Survival is more important.

Then he'll have nothing, then he'll delete the recording. He'll say that I tried to attack him, make up some stupid story. Everything will get lost in Internal Affairs and a cover-up will occur.

This guy's a psycho and if he did this to me, and he's so outgoing and confident and completely unbothered by what he's done, I'm sure he has done it to others.

I have to make him pay for this.

"Give me my phone back," I say.

"No, I don't think so."

He walks over to the bathroom off of the kitchen. I follow him and hear a big splash as the phone drops into the toilet.

"What are you doing?" I snap.

Philip points the gun at my head and tells me to stay back. The phone floats for a few seconds at the top of the water before sinking to the bottom.

"We're going to wait a little bit," he says. "I need that phone to get nice and waterlogged so that no data can be retrieved off of it ever. Just in case. I'm covering the bases. I don't need you to be so smart, Charlotte. I need you to trust me. I'm here to help you solve the case, the three cases to find the killer, and I'm here to remind you to stay quiet about what happened since no one's going to believe you anyway. Stay in your lane. Work here in Palm Valley. Do your little job in your little community. Don't ever think of coming on my turf, into my world. I don't care what your dad says or what he does. He's retiring anyway."

I say nothing.

."It's going to be better after that. He's such a stickler for rules. He likes everything to be done just so. No, I think the FBI needs someone else."

He picks up the phone from the toilet, turns on the faucet, and douses it with water. I watch a torrent rush over it. When he pulls it back out and tries to turn it on, it doesn't work. For good measure, he tosses it under the water again and gives it back to me.

"Okay, you're all set here now. I'll see you back in the office."

29

___

CHARLOTTE

As soon as he leaves, I break down. I hold myself and sob. It's one thing for this to have happened before, but it's another for him to threaten me like this.

I look at the phone on the counter, dripping wet, and I cry, and I try to turn it back on to no avail. As the emotion overcomes me, I take a number of deep breaths to calm down.

"We're going to make this work," I say.

One of these days, he's going to pay for what he did. I don't know how that's going to happen or what I'm going to do to make that happen, but I make a promise to myself that *that* man is not going to do that to anybody else.

Not ever again.

After a quick shower to wash away the mere presence of him, I wrap myself in a towel and walk around with a spray bottle full of bleach to scrub every surface that he touched.

After getting dressed, I grab my phone and toss it into my purse. I head over to the nearest Best Buy. A bored pale teenager with a contorted spine who looks like he has played way too many video games welcomes me to their Genius Bar.

"I need your help. I dropped this phone into water, and I was just wondering if there's anything you can do about it."

He examines it and asks, "How long was it in there?"

"A while. Can you fix it?"

"I don't think we can do much for it. It seems pretty waterlogged," he says when he opens the back.

Anger at Philip transforms into tears that I can't manage to hold back. The teenager is so shocked by my outburst that he actually takes a step away from me.

"I can try to send it off to our team. They sometimes have luck getting these things to work afterward, but I can't promise anything."

"Yes, that'd be great," I say. "Anything you can do."

Of course, I have the resources of the police department at my call, but the truth is that this is a personal matter and I have to treat it as such. Not certain as to what to do next, I walk out to the car and feel the furnace-like heat. The air-conditioning inside is bitter cold and it makes my skin ice. The heat, on the other hand, is comforting and soft, wrapping around me like a forgotten blanket. I have always loved dry heat. The summers get tough reaching highs of 120 degrees Fahrenheit and typically hovering around 110. But it's not summer yet. It's only ninety now with 10% humidity.

If you were to lick your lips and stand in the slight breeze coming off the mountain, your saliva would start to evaporate almost immediately, and you'd feel the coolness of it on your mouth. Instead of going back to my car, I decide to go around to the back of the store. The mountains stretch out in all directions, the shopping center being nestled right at the bottom. There's one small road that goes out back. All the trucks and delivery vehicles come in the other way. The road is something of a throughway and leads to a popular hiking spot.

You can leave your car right along there and head up the rocks of the pine crest trail. The trail is about two miles, but it connects to a whole network of trails heading up almost 10,000 feet in elevation. I hadn't been all the way to the top, not on a hike. That's something you have to really prepare for, leaving at 3:00 a.m. if you want to make it down with the last tram. You can always take the tram up, which has beautiful views of Palm Valley and the high desert mountains on the other side, and it's not uncommon for the peaks to have snow at the top even in April.

It typically stays quite cool up there as well, all throughout the summers. My hike up is much more strenuous. It's ninety-one degrees according to my smart watch, and I'm not even sure if I'm going to be able to make the whole two-mile loop since the initial ascent is quite vertical. But it feels good to get my legs moving.

I take one step in front of another, clamoring and zigzagging up the rocks, making my way in between the boulders. As I hike I notice all the various shades of beige. There are a few creosote bushes, but mostly it's the jagged edges of the rocks that draw my attention. A small breeze comes over the mountain cooling me off, and I realize that I don't have any water with me. It's back in the car.

I'm not going to walk for more than a mile and a half. It's too steep and it's getting too hot, and when I get to the point where I'm about to turn around, I wipe the little bit of sweat off my brow and look down the valley. There's uneven terrain, wild lands, a place where untamed sheep and goats rush at twilight to get away from the mountain lions that stalk them. It's probably what I love most about all of Southern California, and the desert in particular.

We live in the middle of civilization, cloistered away in small towns and safe suburban communities, but the wilderness is right out there just around the corner. I love that. I've loved seeing coyotes wander around my neighborhood. Of course, it's dangerous for the local pets and I hope that their owners have enough sense to make sure the gates to their yards are closed and they are kept safe. I believe the wilderness has a right to exist, and I hope we never forget that we used to be wild as well.

Speaking of coyotes, out in the distance on the ridge, two little ears peek out and study me inquisitively. Her brown coat allows her to blend in well with the boulder next to her. She's sitting in the shade curled up just like any other dog, looking at me with curiosity. I give her space, even though it takes everything in me to not walk over and try to make a friend.

I'm exhausted and feel like I should be sweaty. It's hard to get drenched in the desert, because here you just perspire a little bit and it evaporates almost as soon as it appears. That's why it's so easy to get dehydrated. You don't really sweat in the same way you do in high humidity, and you think that maybe you'll be okay if you go a little bit further. But then you can reach that point of no return where the heat just wraps around you and it's just too much.

I walk back into Best Buy and head straight to their phone counter. I look at the array of phones, grab the newest model of the one that I'm familiar with, and purchase it. I already have everything set up on my cloud account, and the clerk helps me transfer my data over from the other phone.

Thirty minutes later, it's like nothing with Philip ever happened. Unfortunately, the recording never got saved and never got sent, but all of my pictures and old emails are preserved along with a full list of contacts. I don't have much hope for the waterlogged phone and wouldn't be surprised if they couldn't do much to save it.

I call into work, explain that I had to get a new phone, and make up a few white lies, covering up for Philip once again. When I get back to the car, my phone rings. The name that shows up on the front catches me by surprise. I haven't talked to her in a while, so much that I even forgot that I had her number. I look at the screen again trying to decide whether I should answer and stare at the name: *Detective Kaitlyn Carr.*

30

CHARLOTTE

I answer the phone right before it goes to voice mail, "Kaitlyn?"

"Charlotte, we're so glad to reach you," she says.

I can feel her smiling through the phone.

"What's up? How are you?" I ask.

"I'm good. Just wanted to say hi."

I know Kaitlyn from the LAPD, or rather I know *of* her. I met her at a conference after I'd already switched to Palm Valley and we reconnected about working there.

I can tell that she has something specific to talk to me about, but it's a little bit awkward on the phone because, well, we've only really had drinks once and don't know each other very well.

"Hey, listen, I know this is kind of weird," she finally says, "but I just wanted to let you know that I'm in the area. I'm off on a break for about a week, and so I wanted to see if you had time to hang out some time, maybe grab some dinner, talk shop."

Talk shop is a euphemism for work, so she does have something to tell me, to talk to me about.

"Yes, that'd be great," I say. "Things are kind of busy now, but I could probably do it tonight. I'm going up to Quail Lake tomorrow to take care of some things."

I don't go into any more details.

"Yes, tonight will work, perfect. What time are you off?"

"Six," I say.

"I really appreciate this, Charlotte. You don't even know."

I smile, nod, and hang up, looking at the screen again.

What could she have to talk to me about, I wonder.

The day proceeds without much incident, we talk to more people at the apartment complex, get their story straight, write up reports. The APB has returned with nothing and we have no further info on the guy on the motorcycle. The day limps along as I fill it up with paperwork, inching for the opportunity to do some real police work.

I don't share any of this with Will because I don't want to have to explain too much. I'm going to keep the situation with Philip to myself until I can have more proof collected or until maybe the phone comes back salvaged in any way.

I don't have much hope for that, but we'll see. Before I call it quits for the day, I realize that it's going to be overtime if the motorcycle or the driver are found.

The assistant district attorney stops by my desk and asks if I have a minute to speak. Crawford's office is in the next building over. She rarely makes in-person visits like this and mainly relies on phone calls or texts.

"Can we do this later?" I ask. "Maybe Monday?"

"No, absolutely not," she says with a gravely serious expression on her face.

She's dressed in a white blouse and a pair of slacks. The blouse is wrinkled and her hair is unusually disheveled, stringy, and pulled up to the top of her head. Her face has a thin line of sweat and she looks like she has come straight from the gym without showering. This is not the Amy Crawford that I know well.

"Is something wrong?" I ask.

She doesn't answer, and instead walks to one of the interrogation rooms, gesturing for us to follow. Will and I exchange looks.

"Is this a good place to talk?" She looks around. "Is that camera on?"

"No," Will says, "not unless you told someone to record."

"God, no." Amy shakes her head, folding her arms across her chest. "I was at the gym during lunch when my investigator came and told me something very disturbing."

That explains her appearance.

"That must have been a late lunch," Will says with a smirk and a casual smile.

"I go when I can." She shrugs.

"What's wrong, Amy?" I ask.

Will gestures for us to sit down at the table, but none of us do. Instead we huddle almost in a tight circle. She takes a step closer to him, and suddenly I become the third wheel.

"Do you want me to leave?" I ask.

"No," she snaps. "This concerns both of you. Will, tell me about Erin Lowry."

My mouth drops open. The parched feeling that I had earlier during my hike returns, only this time it's because of shock reverberating through my body.

If Amy Crawford knows about Erin-- I don't finish that thought.

"What about her?" Will says, playing dumb.

"*What about her?* You're having a *relationship*. Currently. You were also in that relationship when she was a primary suspect in the murder of her husband. Tell me that's not true."

He takes a step back. His eyes dart around the room, instilling the opposite of confidence.

"You're with her now and you know what else?" She looks at me. "You're expecting a baby with her."

He starts to open his mouth.

"Don't you dare lie to me, Will. My investigator saw you at her OBGYN appointment."

"Why are you following her?"

"Because the defense is following her, you idiot," she snaps. "Because this is a big case. This is a double murder, and one of the victims was pregnant. This is all over the news. They're putting a fricking *Dateline* and a *20/20* episode about this. This is like the super bowl of true crime here. I can either come out as a victorious prosecutor, avenging and getting justice for the murder victims and their families, or this whole department can look like idiots, losers, and corrupt, small-town hicks because of *you.* You were the detective on this case and you were having an affair with a primary suspect."

"It's not an affair. She was not with him. She was divorced," he says.

Amy raises her hand as if to slap him, but Will doesn't flinch. He stares at her and she quickly lowers it.

"I can't believe you did this to me. I thought we were friends."

"I didn't do anything to you," Will says. "Erin and I knew each other from a long time ago. We reconnected. Nothing happened until she was cleared as a suspect."

"But you were helping her. You were her friend."

"So, what? Detectives aren't supposed to have friends?"

"Detectives aren't supposed to be investigating their friends. Yes. You would've been removed from the case, but you didn't want to be because you wanted to help her."

"Because you were all circling in around her. Everyone thought that she did it."

"That's true, we did," she says. "Because she looked like she did, because she was found at the crime scene. She had blood on her. She was stalking them. She was angry. She was a scorned ex-wife."

"She had no memory of what had happened so it's not like she had another story to tell us."

"But we would've found out the truth. Don't you believe in your partner here? Don't you believe-" Then she looks at me, narrowing her eyes.

"Oh my God," she whispers. I clench my jaw. "You knew about this. It's not just him."

"I don't know what you're talking about," I say.

She shakes her head and laughs. "Wow. I'm such an idiot. Of course, you knew about this. You're partners. You're as thick as thieves. Friends till the end, thin blue line, all that crap. Right?"

"I'm not going to say anything else to you." I try to remember all the things they taught us in the academy, in case of an accidental shooting. "You don't talk to anyone until you have our representation. You don't apologize. You don't acknowledge."

"You know what? You don't need to confirm anything. I can see it on your face."

I look away from her. Luckily my face is not exactly proof in court, but I know what she means.

"Erin didn't kill anyone," Will says.

"Yes, I know that. Too bad that I can't prove it now because this whole case is going to get thrown out."

"Why? Because of me?"

"Of course because of you. There's going to be a mistrial. I can make certain arguments about inevitable discovery, but their attorney's good and who the hell knows what they have on you. You messed this up, Will, you and Charlotte both. I don't know if I can get those two people justice after this. And Erin, I don't think she'll ever be cleared, because there'll always be these suspicions, especially given how big the story's going to get now."

"It's not right," I say. "You have to make this right. He was just trying to protect his friend and help her because he knew the truth."

"Whatever," Amy says, pacing from one side of the room to another.

"You have to believe him."

"I want to, I do. Your other work has been above suspicion. You two have always been the two detectives that I never worried about. Never thought would take a dime from the evidence room. Never thought could be corrupted in any way because you were on the straight and narrow. You cared about this job. You cared about doing it right, but this, this is a huge deal. This ruins the whole case. There's going to be a mistrial and the defense, they know all about you. If I participate in this, I'm going to be part of the cover-up."

"I'm so sorry," Will says, "but you have to believe me, Charlotte had nothing to do with this. It was just me. I was just trying to help my friend."

"The mother of your soon-to-be-born child, right?"

"Yes. We were together romantically before when we were teens. The second chance romance, you know how hot those are, but I never let that get in the way. Not of my job. If I thought that she was involved in any way, we wouldn't be together, none of this would be happening."

"So, you're telling me you're not just strategically framing the victim's business partner?"

"No, of course not. Don't you remember what happened?" She looks at me and I almost flinch at the memory.

"None of that was staged. None of that was faked. They did that on their own," Will says. "I just knew that Erin didn't do this and I was trying to help her find out what happened. If I had come forward, they would have taken the case away from me and probably Charlotte, too, and assigned it to those other detectives who shall remain unnamed."

Amy exhales. She knows exactly who he means, the ones that everyone knows aren't exactly on the up and up.

"You know that, though there's no proof of anything, those two guys are shady, for sale. They get what they want, and they get their results, but at a cost," Will continues to plead. "You can't really believe half of those jailhouse snitches. You know that."

"I've used those jailhouse snitches to get convictions," Amy admits.

"Yes, to confirm what you thought you already knew, but you wouldn't depend on them for the whole case, right?" Will asks. "You know that they will say pretty much anything that any prosecutor wants them to."

"What are you getting at, Will, exactly?" Amy finally asks.

"I don't know." He takes a long pause. "I guess what I'm trying to say is that I'm sorry."

"Fine. Let's just hope that I don't get a mistrial."

"Is that possible?" I ask.

"Perhaps," Amy says with a deep sigh. "But it's not going to be easy."

31

CHARLOTTE

K aitlyn and I meet up at a little bit of an upscale restaurant called Lemon in downtown Palm Valley. I suggested it because the atmosphere is very girly. They serve cucumber martinis and have décor that's a mixture of pink and green. I am craving something very much the opposite of my life at this moment and think this would be a good place for her to go especially given the fact that she is on vacation.

"Oh my God. What is this place?" She smiles, looking around.

When we sit down and order a round of cocktails, the menu is filled with trendy appetizers. The tables are marble squares with brushed brass legs. The walls are surrounded by *Golden Girls* inspired bright floral and tropical wallpaper.

"This place is amazing," Kaitlyn says as we clink our glasses and thanks me for inviting her.

"I haven't been to a place like this for a while and I figured you're on a trip, I wanted to show you the good life out here in the desert."

"Just so chic and cool. This cocktail is already blowing my mind." She smiles. "How do you like living out here?"

"To tell you the truth, it's pretty awesome. It's like everything good about Los Angeles. No traffic for one, but same great restaurants and people. Much cheaper, too. Have you been here before?"

She shakes her head no. Her hair falls a little in her face and she's wearing just a little bit of makeup to make her eyes pop. Her nails are medium length, painted a cool blue. Her fingers are adorned with oversized turquoise rings on one hand and three stackable rings on the other.

"I've just been out here once or twice before but I haven't spent any serious time. That's why I came out for about a week."

"Well, you're going to love it," I say. "It's pretty awesome and I'm really happy I made the move."

"Oh, yes. Different than the LAPD?"

"For sure. The pace is a lot slower. I mean, we work long hours as well, especially deputies on the street, but there's a lot less crime and the politics aren't exactly the same."

"What do you mean by that?" she asks.

I can't tell if she's just being mildly curious or if she's seriously asking me advice on what it's like to live here.

I take a couple of sips of my cucumber martini and at this very moment realize just how much I have missed having a girlfriend presence in my life. I have a few women that I know from work, but they have families, other friendships, and it's hard to make time.

"I like my lieutenant a lot," I say. "He gives me a lot of leeway, I like having autonomy. I don't have to report back about every single moment, about every single thing that I do. My partner is good, too."

I don't mention the fact that he might lose his badge. We haven't gotten that close yet, but maybe in a few more drinks.

"How are you doing? How's the LAPD treating you?"

"I'm taking a bit of a break after my sister's disappearance and everything that happened. It was hard to go back to business as usual. I'm trying to reevaluate what to do with my life."

"And, any conclusions?"

"Yes. My fiancé is arguing for me to follow my passion but I'm a cop, I don't even know what that means."

I laugh. "Congratulations on your engagement."

"He's an FBI agent, so who knows?" she jokes.

I smile. I remember, from the one time that we met, her dry sense of humor and how much I enjoyed that. She's really good at being self-deprecating because that's kind of an unusual thing nowadays. When you make fun of yourself people think that you just have bad self-esteem. I guess it only works for those with an English accent.

"Is your fiancé here, too?"

"He's here on a work thing, but yes, technically. But he's retiring soon. Well, not retiring, quitting, I guess is a better way of putting it."

"He's not gonna do it anymore?" I ask.

"No, he's not really cut out for it. He doesn't really like it, had some issues in the department. But I'm actually considering going into the academy."

"You want to be an FBI agent?"

"Not totally decided yet, but I'm looking for a way out. That's why I called you. You're the only person I know who took off. Did their own thing. You didn't like the way things were at the LAPD and you said, 'Fine. I'm going to go out on my own.'"

"Well, not exactly on my own," I say. "I mean, I just went to work for another department."

"Yes, but still. I'm just feeling overwhelmed with everything. It's been hard."

"About your sister?"

"Yes. It was just a very stressful time. Just made me realize how much good I can do helping people find their loved ones."

"Well, if you're looking for a less stressful time, I'm not sure the FBI is it."

"There's a behavioral unit," she says. "I've always been into psychology."

I nod slightly.

"Sorry, I don't mean to put all this on you. This is supposed to be a nice meeting, just catching up on old times."

"Well, the thing is that," I smile, "we never really had old times. We met once. But feel free to talk to me about anything you want."

"Sometimes, I do think about transferring. I wanted to ask you about what it's like to live here."

"It's great. To be honest, it's much cheaper being on the coast. The summers are tough, but you get used to them much faster than you think. It's just hot, and then it's just more hot, but it doesn't even matter. You can always go out, get your exercise and fresh air in the mornings when it's in the 80s. You can get a lot more house here than you can in LA. I have a three bedroom with a pool and an office. It's very spacious. It's a little bit too much for me, but given the crappy apartment I had on Wilshire, I like it. It's clean. People are still LA people, so you've got the nice restaurants. You've got diversity. You've got friendliness. As far as the job goes, it's a little bit less intense. I mean, you still put in a lot of hours when things happen, but there are just not as many criminals. There's just not as much going on, so you can focus your efforts on community outreach, that kind of thing."

"What about the murders that just happened?" she asks.

"You mean the boys? There's one here. One up in the high desert and another one that went missing," I say. "I'm surprised that you heard about it."

"It was on the news."

"Well, of course, crime happens."

"What do you think happened?" Kaitlyn asks.

"I think the cases are related. Probably one guy. I'm uncertain about calling him a serial killer, but the M.O. matches. Everything matches, except for one thing."

"What is that?"

"Well, the last one. He wasn't found. Not his body, not the boy. We're all hoping that he's still alive."

"Of course," she says.

Our food arrives. Little portions on clean white square plates. My bite melts in my mouth.

"Wow, this food is delicious. So fresh and yummy. Didn't think fish would be this fresh in the desert."

"Please. It's all very boujee around here." I smile.

She laughs, tossing her short hair to one side.

"I like your haircut," I say. "It really fits you, short like that."

"Thanks." She smiles. "Thought I'd try something new. Not sure I like it, but it will always grow out, right?"

I nod. "You know, you look the same from when I saw you. A little better even."

We have a little bit of food and chitchat about the comparisons between LA and Palm Valley more. Then suddenly out of the blue, she says, "I actually have something else to talk to you about."

I nod and wait for her to reply.

"I got this call from someone who supposedly has some knowledge about what happened to that boy. It's unclear, but I think it has something to do with your case."

32

CHARLOTTE

She puts a strawberry in her mouth, and I stare at her. Did I really hear her say what I just thought that she said?

"What are you talking about?" I ask. "You got a call?"

She nods her head and smiles.

"Okay, before you get too excited, I can't make any promises about it, but yes, I got a call. That's one of the reasons I'm here."

"What kind of call?" I ask.

"About your case. It was on my personal number, belonged to a woman. She sounded like she was maybe in her 60s or 70s. It was hard to tell because she had the low raspy voice of a smoker."

"Okay." I nod.

"She asked me to confirm that I was who I said I was."

"What do you mean by that?"

"She just asked if I'm Detective Kaitlyn Carr, with the LAPD. I said yes. She said that she had something very important to tell me, but she can't give me her name or any other information."

"What did she say?"

"She said that there were two boys who went missing on their bicycles in Mesquite County. She said they were killed, and their bodies were found. She knows who did it, but she can't tell me. She said that one is now missing, and she's not sure if he's alive."

"Who is this?" I ask.

"I have no idea."

"What else did she say? Why did she call you?"

"She said that she read about my sister's case and that she's located in LA County. She said that she wanted to reach out to me because I would understand."

I nod, not fully understanding anything. "Does she know who did this?"

"Yes, but she's not saying who. It's probably a family friend, a relative, maybe her son. She said that he can't stop doing what he was doing. She read his journals, and she has them. As soon as she found out that it was him, she looked up the news, and it matched up with what he wrote. She just couldn't let it go, she couldn't come forward, but she's not coming forward."

I say, "She reached out to you. You're not even working this case."

"I know, but she sounded scared. Her voice was all frazzled. She had a cough fit in the middle. It sounded like she has asthma, or is using an oxygen tank. She's not in good shape."

"Where did she call from? Did you trace her phone?"

"I tried. I got in touch with the cell phone company, but nothing. It went back to a payphone in West Hollywood, but there's a lot of them there."

"Seriously? Pay phones are still around?"

"Yes. The area still has a large elderly population. Some lobbied to keep the phones because they just have landlines and don't know how to use cells. The city liked the excuse to not bother taking them out yet. There were no cameras pointing at the phone. I have no way of finding out who did this, or who called."

"Did you get the location of the payphone?"

"Yes. It was near a park. I even talked to the business owners in the area to try to get their CCTV but didn't see anything significant."

"When did all of this happen?"

"It was a slow couple of days, and I was working on this case, in addition to my paperwork. I wanted to come to you with something, not just this strange phone call from this woman. Unfortunately, I don't have anything, I have no idea who she is."

"But she knows who *he* is."

"Yes."

"She has access to his journals. Wait, that probably means that he lives with her," I say.

"At least part of the time, I'm assuming. I have no idea." Kaitlyn shrugs.

"Why would he come all the way here to commit these crimes?"

"I guess he's one of those few criminals who are following the rules about not crapping where you eat. Without this phone call, you'd never look in LA County."

"There's an APB out on the motorcycle," I say.

"There is?"

"Yes, we got a video, and a partial plate, came up with a name, but I don't have any idea who he is."

"Do you happen to have a picture just in case?" she says.

"Sure." I pull it up on my phone. Keith Moraine, and then her face falls.

"What, what is it?"

"I know him," she says.

———

"HOW DO YOU KNOW HIM?"

"He's my neighbor's son," she says.

"Are you sure?"

"Yes. I never made the connection, but she's a heavy smoker as well. The caller's voice was a little bit altered, like it was being filtered through something. I guess I should have figured that I might know her. I've seen him a few times. He came to visit. Just passing by, but he didn't have a Harley. Are you sure that this was a Harley?"

"Yes," I say. "What else?"

"He lives up in the high desert, in Apple Valley. He visits sometimes. He seemed friendly enough. Bringing his mom groceries, that kind of thing, taking her to the doctor."

I suddenly notice that I'm holding a piece of bread in my hand. I had taken a bite of it, but that was a while ago. I'm hanging on to every word that she says.

"That's probably why she called me when she found the journals and saw the documents and the news. She thought that I could help, but she didn't want to turn him over or anything like that. We have to talk to her."

"Yes, for sure," I say. "Does she scare easily?" I ask.

"Yes. I mean, I'm not sure. She's kind of a hard read. She used to be a teacher for years, so she doesn't take crap from people, not easily."

"But she's trying to help us, that's something. Did she mention specifics about the journals or anything like that?"

"Just details about the cases that she could have gotten from the news, but she's not the kind to create waves to seek attention. She's the opposite of that. We have to believe her."

"So she must be telling the truth."

"Yes, I would say so."

We get everything arranged with our departments and I follow her out to LA in my car.

33

CHARLOTTE

Will is on temporary leave now, so I go myself. I follow Kaitlyn out to LA with my own car. I have strict instructions from the lieutenant to report on every detail as soon as I get it, not to make any of my own decisions after the interview. Meanwhile, as I drive over, the department is running all sorts of checks on Mrs. Moraine. When I get there, I get an update.

"Yes, she is Keith Moraine's mother," the lieutenant says. "There is a Harley motorcycle registered in his name and the partial plate matches. It's him. How you conduct this interview, it's going to be of utmost importance. We want her to lead us to him but we don't want to scare her."

He goes on and on, telling me all the things that I already know. Yes, it's a delicate situation. Yes, there's a lot to balance. Of course, there is. I know that, but I have to rely on my own intuition as well. I can't have everything planned out.

Kaitlyn and I decide to go to speak to her at her home rather than bring her in. This is part and parcel of making her feel comfortable. Mrs. Moraine lives downstairs from Kaitlyn's small one-bedroom apartment. I ask her how much she pays in rent and she says $2,400. I tell her about my mortgage and her mouth nearly drops.

"You seriously pay $2,500 for a three-bedroom, a pool, and a yard and it already appreciated $100,000? Okay, I hate you. I never want to see you again," she jokes as we search for parking on a busy street.

"Look, there's perks to living here as well. You can walk to that restaurant down there, to that club up the street, to the Grove. That's nice. That's what I miss about LA."

"Yes? What about the traffic? Do you miss that?" she asks.

"No, definitely not. We got lucky coming in this morning but that's because it was eleven. We squeaked in after the morning rush and before the afternoon rush, which starts at noon." She laughs.

"Listen, thank you so much for doing this," I tell her right before we get to the apartment. "You're on your vacation and you didn't have to come and find me and tell me all this right away. I just really appreciate it. If there's anything I can do to reciprocate, let me know."

"Of course. This is what the best of law enforcement is about, right? Cooperation."

"Yes, but doing it on your time off, that's something else."

"Don't worry, I'm getting paid overtime for this." She smiles and gives me a wink.

I shake my head and chuckle to myself.

Mrs. Moraine's apartment is cluttered, filled with all sorts of memorabilia or rather crap from who knows where. It's like a thrift store that needs to be cleaned out of stuff that never got bought, but I'm sure that they all have sentimental value to her and a story to go with each piece.

There's a collection of old bottles all over the dining room table and *National Geographics* as well as bundles of other magazines in piles. She wouldn't exactly qualify for the A&E show about hoarding, but she's on her way there. Give it five more years and you won't be able to walk through this place without climbing the walls.

At first, Kaitlyn makes small talk with Mrs. Moraine, introducing me as her friend before coming clean.

"I'm actually here to talk to you about something very important," she says. "I know that you called me from a payphone about your son and I want to talk to you about that."

Mrs. Moraine's mouth drops open. She's an older woman, a little bit overweight, dressed in a bright yellow blouse and beige slacks. She looks like she has just come from the farmers market. There is a basket of flowers sitting on the dining room table. She folds her hands across her lap and looks up at Kaitlyn, and then to me.

"You're Detective Charlotte Pierce."

I nod.

"I saw you on the news. I wondered if I should call you instead."

"Can you tell me about these journals that you found?"

"They belong to my son," she says. "He detailed what he wanted to do, and then he did it. I have them here but I want you to promise me that he's not going to get hurt."

I hesitate for a moment. "I'm not sure what that means exactly."

"I don't want him to get shot during the arrest," she says.

"Of course not."

"Yes? I'm not so sure." She tilts her head.

Her hair is in large, thick curls. The way that the sun hits it, I realize that it's a wig. There's something that's unreal about it, reminding me of the kind of hair that Barbie has, a little bit too lustrous, especially given her age.

"We're going to take our utmost care with this situation. Your son is innocent until proven guilty. We both take that very seriously."

"Yes, maybe *you* do but what about the other cops? What if he has a gun?"

"If he has a gun, it's a completely different matter, Mrs. Moraine. You know that, right?"

She hesitates and shuts down.

"A child is missing," I say. "His name is Ari Gomez. Do you have any idea where he could be?"

"I can't tell you anything until I have some sort of immunity situation."

"Mrs. Moraine," Kaitlyn says. "There will not be immunity. You will never get immunity for helping your son in this matter. In fact, you can be tried as an accessory if something happens to that child."

"If he's even still alive," she says.

"You don't think that he is?"

My heart sinks.

She shakes her head. "I have no idea. All I know is that I found the journals. That's all I want to talk about."

"Where did you find them? Can you show them to us?" Kaitlyn asks.

Mrs. Moraine nods. She walks in the back room and then brings them out. They're in boxes. Keith has neat handwriting. Not all caps, but incredibly readable. A bit in cursive, but the letters are rounded and fat and easy to decipher.

She points to the dates of the entries, which correspond to when the children were killed. My heart starts to beat uncontrollably. The names and locations written in latitude and longitude coordinates match up exactly when I put the locations into Google.

"This is exactly where they were found," I tell Kaitlyn.

"So, he really did it?" Mrs. Moraine asks us.

We nod.

"Has he ever done something like this before?" I ask her.

She shrugs and shakes her head.

"Keith travels for work a lot. He's a district manager. He visits me, but he flies all around the West Coast. He just happened to bring over a bunch of his stuff because he and his wife are getting divorced, and he put it into my spare room. He rented an apartment up in Apple Valley near his kids, but the lease doesn't start for a little while and he didn't want to pay for a storage unit."

Mrs. Moraine continues to speak, looking somewhere out in the distance. I feel bad for her. This is her son after all, but I appreciate her telling us anything that she can.

"I love my son," Mrs. Moraine says with tears in her eyes. "Please don't confuse this with anything other than that. I want to help him and I don't want him to hurt anyone else."

34

CHARLOTTE

Kaitlyn and I drive up to Apple Valley, which is about an hour and a half north of LA to the address that Mrs. Moraine gave us. A deputy stays with her and makes sure that she doesn't make any calls to warn her son about our presence and doesn't change her mind about helping us. I'm pretty sure that she won't, but of course, anything can happen and we have to take certain precautions.

We arrive at a nondescript two-story apartment building at the end of a busy street next to a strip mall, nothing fancy, but not too tragic either. There's no motorcycle out front, no car in his assigned parking spot, and no one at the house. We look around uncertain as to how long we should wait.

"I hadn't thought this through," I admit to Kaitlyn and she just shrugs shifting her weight from one foot to another.

We look to see if anyone is coming, walking around, but no one is here.

"I guess we better go to the local police department to let them know what we're doing," I say. "Maybe they can put someone here to watch for him."

"The APB is already out," Kaitlyn says. Now it's my turn to shrug. "But I guess we should."

The nearest police station is less than two miles away. My phone rings when I pull into a parking spot.

"We found his bike!" Will says. "By the side of the freeway!"

"Where?"

"Here, right near Desert Hills."

"Is anyone there?" I ask.

"No. He must've walked off."

"Is the bike damaged?"

"No. Maybe ran out of gas, maybe he just dropped it because he knew that we're onto him. I have no idea. I'm not really in any operational capacity as you know, but I heard through the grapevine and wanted to let you know."

"Thanks. The lieutenant is going to be calling. If he does, don't tell him that you know."

"Yes, sure, of course."

I don't bother when I relay the news to Kaitlyn, and we agree that we can't waste any time with the police department here. We can just call them on the way and notify them.

"I've got to get back. I'm actually probably going to leave you here," she says. "It's a long drive back there and I already brought my stuff back."

"Yeah, that's probably best," I say. "Sorry about your trip though."

"No, I'm glad that I could help you out with everything."

"I'm glad we took our two cars." I smile.

"Yes, whose nice suggestion was that?" she jokes since it's clearly hers.

I tilt my head back and I shake my head at her a little bit laughing at her pompousness. We promise to stay in touch and I tell her that I'll definitely keep her updated about whatever happens with this case.

"You should still take a little break. Don't forget to relax," I say. "Don't just jump right into the next project."

"When are you going to listen to your own advice?"

She smiles and gets into her car. I arrive back in Palm Valley, exhausted, but in a good way, excited as well. There's finally a break. The motorcycle is still by the side of the road as I had the lieutenant leave it there for me to look at before the Crime Scene Investigation took it away.

Why did he drop it?

Why did he leave it?

Who tipped him off about the APB?

It might've been his mom, of course, but I doubt that. The journals that she showed us were pretty dark and grim detailing all of his dreams and desires of what he wanted to do to the kids.

Then there's the documentation of how he felt when he took them. He admitted to shooting them, but he did say that he held back on sexually assaulting them because he knew that would be wrong. The last kid, however, Ari Gomez, I'm not sure if he had been as lucky. His body has still not been found, and I'm losing hope that he's alive.

The motorcycle is relatively new, well taken care of, no scuff marks anywhere, pristine and clean. CSI have already brushed for fingerprints and other information and I'm certain that it will be a match since he is the owner. The way that the deputies are joking around in their car tells me they've been here for a while. There could be worse posts to be assigned to, but I'm not in the mood to waste people's time.

"Has anyone gone down this road?" I ask them.

They nod their heads. "Yes. About forty-five minutes in and out. There's one house there. We spoke to the man who owns it. Didn't see anyone, didn't fit the description."

"And who spoke to him?"

"I did," one of the deputies says. He's in his early 30s, not as much of a joker as his friend. I've seen his reports and they've all been detailed and well-written.

"Did he have any cameras up?" I ask. He shakes his head. "He seemed like something of a technophobe. Still had an old TV in there, the ones with the bunny ears. The only phone that I saw was a landline with one of those thick curls attached to it."

"Wow. He really doesn't like technology."

"Yeah. Not at all. A VCR with a big videotape collection of movies, so not sure he even has streaming internet in that cabin."

"How old is he?"

"Probably in his sixties." He shrugs.

"Didn't tell him much, but he said he didn't see anyone walking on foot and he would, too, because it's the only place anyone would walk past."

"Yes, okay." I nod. I guess that settles that.

I look around for tracks in the sagebrush and see nothing. It's hot, the clouds are in cotton ball bunches drifting across the sky. The air is still, which is a rare thing by the side of the freeway. This is the windy quarter where the wind sweeps in between the mountains and come through in roaring gusts. Not too far away from here are rows and rows of giant windmills harnessing the power of all of the wind and providing much-needed electricity to the valley.

As I walk away from the deputy and a little bit up the hill, I step on weeds of sagebrush and look out into the distance where my eye reaches further and further back until I lose myself in the horizon that meets the sky.

Missing Lives

My eyes wander along the ridge. I can feel the shallowness of my breath. I decide to drive out, but the deputy stops me.

"It's really quite a long way, ma'am, and I doubt that he'll say anything else. I know you just drove out from LA, so I'm just trying to warn you."

"Thanks, I appreciate that."

The CSI team comes back asking if it's okay for them to take the bike. I nod. I make a quick phone call to the lieutenant and then head back home. I did the most that I could, right?

They already got a witness statement. I saw no footprints anywhere. I have no idea if anyone had seen anything at all, and so tomorrow we'll fight another day. It'll be another battle, but today I'll get some rest. This is what I say to myself as I get into bed.

This is what I have with the best of my intentions, but of course, my subconscious mind has other thoughts and motivations. I can't fall asleep. I can't stop my mind from racing.

After a little while, about three hours in, I no longer bother. I open my eyes and decide that I have to go. I have to find out for myself if Moraine had made his way past that house.

I get dressed, grab my things, start the engine and drive off.

35

CHARLOTTE

The town is quiet at night, and the desert is even quieter. The paved parts of the town are surrounded by miles and miles of wilderness. There are people who still live in homesteader cabins, little shacks, or old houses that they inherited from their family members. In the 1950s, the government tried to populate this county by giving out free five-acre plots in exchange for cultivating and building a small cabin. Outside of Palm Valley and some developed parts of the town, there are plenty of places where you can still buy small plots of land for ten to twenty-thousand dollars.

It's pitch dark now and I use only my headlights to illuminate the way. I brought a flashlight in a backpack, as I've done a little bit of hiking on my own, and they always came in handy. Out here, there's so little light pollution that the milky way spreads in all directions and the moon shines brightly providing a lot of light.

My eyes wander along the ridge. Ever since this place was a frontier, the ridge was where you could see someone walk for miles. After visiting large cities on the East Coast, I quickly forgot just how close to the west this world is. The little place I call home. There are junipers growing just beyond the ridge and broken boulders dotting the ridge itself. People from the past have taken shelter under these junipers to protect them from the harsh sun during the day and to provide a little bit of coziness during the grueling winter winds at night.

Driving down an access road, I see a cabin out in the distance. I park and make my way on foot, walking slowly making no sudden movements. Following the road, but not exactly along it, hiding myself just a little bit out of sight, I notice the way that my weight shifts as I make my way forward from one foot to another. The ground is uneven.

The light is on and I approach slowly knowing that in these parts, it's common for people to keep a rifle by the door. Especially if this man doesn't have a Nest camera or anything else to show him who's outside.

I knock a few times.

A few moments later, I hear him walking over, pushing something that rattles behind him. When he opens the door, I realize that it's his oxygen tank. He breathes in slowly and exhales. It reminds me distinctly of scuba diving and how the only sound you hear under the water is of your own breath.

"Excuse me, sir. My name is Detective Charlotte Pierce. I wanted to ask you about a case that I'm working on."

"In the middle of the night?"

"Yes, it's of utmost importance. There's a child who's missing and in grave danger. We believe that the owner of the motorcycle that was abandoned by the freeway made his way down here."

"How do you imagine he did that? I already talked to one of your deputies before."

"Yes. I know, sir. Mr. Whitlock." I correct myself, insinuating to him that I know his name and that this is a follow-up rather than a first contact conversation.

Over the years, I've noticed that this puts people at ease. They don't feel like they have to repeat everything they have said, but they also sometimes slip up and say things they don't exactly mean to say.

"You think this guy abandoned his bike and walked all this way? Didn't it take you forty-five minutes to drive down in your car?" he asks and then inhales and exhales loudly.

I nod. "Yes, it did. I don't know how exactly he got here, but I'm asking you if you have seen anyone or anything suspicious at all today."

"No, I haven't. I already told the other cop that. I also told him that I don't want to be bothered. I was quite rude so I'm assuming that he shared that news with you."

Mr. Whitlock is a heavy-set man with a receding hairline. He doesn't invite me inside. Looking over his flannel shirt, I see the rows and rows of VHS tapes that the deputy was talking about as well as the tiny TV positioned right in front of the couch.

"Would you mind if I took a look around?"

"My house? Yes, I would mind," Mr. Whitlock says. "I want you to leave. Of course, I don't want no little kids to be harmed so if I see someone, I will call and let you know. Do you have a card or something?"

I reach into my pocket and hand it to him.

"Thank you, Ms. Pierce. I'll be in touch."

He closes the door in my face, just as I'm about to say something else. I inhale deeply and decide to take a moment to walk around his property, nevertheless. I'm not sure if he has five acres or two or twenty, but he knows that I'm here so he's probably not going to shoot me. As for that rifle by the door, I was right about it. When I glanced down at his tank, I saw the butt of it waiting for its chance to frighten an intruder.

His house is nestled next to a group of giant boulders. The desert makes a crunchy sound underneath my black and white sneakers with a thick sole. I had some issues with the ball of my foot after pedaling my bike too hard one day. I couldn't step on it at all. Wincing from pain and unwilling to wait two months for the podiatrist appointment, I went to a local foot store that specializes in selling shoes for old people and they recommended this shoe line. Chunky and not at all my style but I do have to admit that they're the most comfortable shoes I probably ever owned. Eventually, my foot started to heal but the shoes remained, especially for long walks like this.

I make my way around the house looking for... God knows what I'm looking for. The boy? Something suspicious?

Everything about Mr. Whitlock is suspicious except that he is the owner of this house. That's how he's listed in an online search and his driver's license, and he has no record. He also has no connection to Keith Moraine or his motorcycle.

Being here is just a hunch anyway and hunches can go either way. Sometimes they're right, sometimes they're not. Tomorrow, Will is going to laugh at me for going all the way out here again wasting my time, especially if Mr. Whitlock calls it in and complains that I'm harassing him or trespassing on his property. Judging by his personality, it seems like a very likely outcome.

Still, I continue to look. I walk all around, a few times even yelling out Ari's name, just for good measure. Not too loud because I don't want Mr. Whitlock to hear, but loud enough that if someone was around, within earshot, he would respond. Eventually, I give up, get back in the car, and consider going back.

I should go back. It's the only thing that makes sense. I should just get in the car, drive home, and call it a day.

I did more than enough work on this case today and I have plenty to write in my report but something keeps me going.

Call it anxiety, call it uncertainty, call it a hunch or intuition. I get in the car and I drive further. Moraine couldn't have disappeared into thin air. He went *somewhere*. Of course, it's utterly possible that someone helping him had picked him up on the freeway and they just took off but still, I continue to drive. If nothing else, I'll at least have a nice drive through the countryside.

The road is bumpy, unpaved, and uneven. It shakes the car around and I can't go more than five miles an hour without feeling like I'm killing the suspension.

More cabins appear. These are dilapidated. They are someone's homes from long ago windswept and forgotten. Perhaps, put up for sale and never sold? There're plenty of these homesteader cabins all around the desert. It's easier to just get a new plot of land instead of dealing with taking down an old cabin and rebuilding on the same foundation. The foundation is probably crap anyway.

Still, despite knowing what I know, I get out in front of every cabin and make my way around. I go into the ones that I can, looking through the open windows and walking through doorless doorways. Just like an abandoned house, dilapidated and out of commission in the city, these cabins are an ideal location for rape and murder because they provide privacy.

This is a perfect place to hold a child hostage. You don't even need to keep them quiet. He can scream and scream until his vocal cords give out but he's not going to be heard because no one is around except for crows, coyotes, and mountain goats, and they're not talking.

I check five cabins. As my search goes further and further toward the mountains, I drink one full bottle of water and refill it from a gallon that I had brought for this exact purpose. It's a warm evening, t-shirt weather, and the winds are light but nevertheless present and still I can't shake the feeling of dread that fills me.

With every cabin, I pray that I don't spot anyone and that everything I'm doing here is for nothing, just a crazy detective with too much time on her hands searching where only ghosts live and yet I continue the search.

Out in the juniper, I see another ridge. I get in the car and drive again. The utility road runs out. I'm off-road completely following marks made by another vehicle. It's not uncommon for people to go joyriding. This is a prime location for that as well. No one around, no one to bother you, beautiful. I see it a lot and there're more than a few accidents and so I follow the tread marks in a spot.

I make my way a little bit further and realize that this car, a regular sedan, is not going to be able to make it very far out here and has a strong possibility of getting stuck. Then as I make my way around the turn, I see a black Jeep. My heart speeds up. I grab my phone, no reception.

Crap. I try to turn around hoping that he won't see me, hoping to have the element of surprise. I slow down and come to a stop. It's probably someone joyriding or maybe teenagers making out.

No one is around the car. I open the door and exit, taking my phone with me. There's no reception but I have a full charge. I can still take pictures which I do, capturing the license plate.

I walk a little bit out of the way and then step on a loud, dry piece of bark that cracks in half.

"No, no, go away!" a faint voice belonging to a kid yells out. "Just leave me alone."

For a second, I wonder if I'm hearing things that I shouldn't.

"Hello?" I yell out.

"Hello, who is this?"

"Hello, this is Detective Charlotte Pierce. I'm going to help you!"

"Come, I'm over here!" the boy yells, his voice is stronger now, louder.

"I'm down underneath in a hole!" he yells.

I keep walking toward the voice and realize what he means. There's a mine shaft right over there. I kneel down, point my flashlight, and I see the top of his head. He shields his eyes with his hand as he looks up.

"Help me!" he yells.

36

CHARLOTTE

"Everything's going to be okay," I say, leaning down over the mineshaft.

The little boy squints as he looks up at me. I point the flashlight away from his eyes and around the deep well.

"Are you okay?"

Ari confirms his name and age and begins to whimper.

"He took me from my bike. He just grabbed me and brought me here. I'm so cold. Can you please help? He's going to come back soon. I don't want to go down into the tunnel."

The county is littered with old, abandoned mineshafts. This place used to be somewhere people would go out, get claims, and build. They would make giant holes in the ground and try to find something of value. Most gave up since the majority were fruitless, but the shafts remained. Occasionally a hiker or two will fall into one breaking their leg. But the rest of the time, they just sit abandoned, as if waiting to be visited.

"How did he get you down here? Was it Keith? Mr. Moraine?" I ask, not sure how he would have introduced himself.

"I don't know."

"The guy who took you on the motorcycle, is he the one who did this?"

"Yes, he was." Ari nods. "He took me here and he had a ladder. I climbed down. He said I had to do it or he would shoot me like those other boys, but he didn't want to. He wanted to save my life. He was doing it to help me."

None of this makes sense.

"He comes and he brings me food and water. He told me that I could go further into the mineshaft and then I could just get lost and die if I don't want to stay here. I don't want to do that."

"Of course not," I say. "I'm going to help you."

"Please don't leave," Ari says as I pull away from him.

"I'm going to leave you the flashlight," I say, dropping it down.

He doesn't catch it, but luckily, it doesn't break. He just has to push the button on the side. Fumbling around for a bit, he finally manages to turn it on.

"I don't have a way to get you, but I have something that I can make into a rope in the car. Okay?"

He nods.

"I'll be right back."

I rush to my car glancing at the Jeep, knowing that it can't have a good reason for being here.

Who does it belong to? Where's the driver?

When I walk past it again I suddenly see *him*, asleep on the passenger side. Sweat runs down my back and my hands turn to ice.

It's Keith Moraine. How did I miss him before?

Without wasting a minute, I rush to my car and open the glove box. My heart starts to race and so does my mind but I force myself to focus.

Do I get the kid out first? No. I need to secure Moraine. I check the door. It's unlocked. I knock, and he rouses.

As soon as I shine the flashlight in his face, I yell, "Police! Get your hands up right now or I'm going to blow your head off!"

He puts them up. I point my gun stabilizing the barrel with my left hand. I grab the door and swing it open.

"Get out of the car!"

"What are you doing here?"

I repeat myself, pulling the blanket off of him to make sure that he has no weapon.

"What are you doing with that boy?"

"He's fine. He's right over there," Moraine says.

"How long are you planning on keeping him there?"

"As long as it takes."

"For what?" I ask.

"For all of this to go away."

"For what to go away?" I snap. "His parents are looking for him. We're all looking for him. Put your hands on the front of the car."

I keep a good distance, a decent distance away from him to make sure that he doesn't hurt me with a kick or anything like that.

I grab my handcuffs.

As I slide one on one of his wrists, he turns to face me and reaches for the gun. I press the trigger. His head blows off.

"Crap," I whisper under my breath.

Blood and brains are everywhere.

"Charlotte." The boy's voice.

The boy yells at the top of his lungs. He begins to cry. Then he says my name over and over again through his sobs.

"It's okay!" I yell back when I get a hold of myself.

"Everything's fine. I'm going to get you out of there."

I rush back to the car. Instead of running to my car and gathering a couple of t-shirts to tie into a knot like a prison escapee from the 1940s, I check the Jeep and luckily find the exact drop-down ladder that he used to get the boy down there.

I drop it over the fence.

"Watch out, ladder is coming down."

The ladder unfurls with force as gravity pulls it down and I hold onto the top securely. To make sure that it's safe, I put a stake into each side and drive them into the ground and then hold onto it.

"Climb up. I'm holding it."

"What happened with the gunshot? Did you shoot someone?"

"Yes," I say. "The bad guy in the Jeep."

Ari lets out a sigh of relief. He climbs upward slowly, not knowing what to do with the flashlight, holding it in one hand as he climbs.

"It's better if you put it in your mouth, in between your teeth, or you can just put it in your pocket. It will fit."

"Okay," he says quietly.

About halfway up, he says that he's scared. I lean over to his side extending my hand.

"You're okay. I'm here. Everything's going to be okay."

When he climbs over, I pull him into my arms and give him a warm hug, checking him for bruises, none of which are visible.

"Are you okay? Did he hurt you besides putting you down there?"

"No, he didn't," he says. "But he said that I had to be down there because he couldn't stop thinking about me, and this was the only way."

"I'm so sorry, honey." I wrap myself around him.

I pull him closer. I put him in the front seat because he refuses to let go of my hand. He wants to sit in the driver's seat so he can cling on to me, but I need to be able to drive. I try to shield him from looking over at the dead body, but it doesn't quite work and he begins to whimper.

"Is that the guy who did this to you?"

"Yes."

"Did he take you from his motorcycle?"

He nods.

"You're okay now."

"You just killed him?" he asks so point-blank, catching me by surprise.

Ari's covered in dust. His mouth is dry and he hasn't been drinking enough. I give him my water, and he drinks all of it. His hair is shaggy, long, and he looks exactly like he did in his pictures.

"I'm going to get you home to your parents as soon as I can, but we've got a bit of a drive back and the roads are not paved here."

"It's okay," he says quietly. "I understand. I'm just happy to be out."

"I tried to put my handcuffs on him," I explain. "Take him back, arrest him, make sure that he had a trial, but he attacked me. He tried to grab the gun out of my hand and I had to shoot him."

"It's okay. He probably would've kept doing it," he says. "He's one of those bad guys that Mom told me about."

"I'm so sorry, sweetie," I say, holding him tighter. "You're safe now. I have you."

We drive down the bumpy road in silence for a while with the moon above us.

"How did he take you?" I ask.

"He just grabbed me when I was riding around in front of my apartment, in front of my house. I should have listened to my mom and not have gone so far, but it's the smallest space, and I like riding my bike as fast as I can. He didn't even say anything to me when he grabbed me. He just walked over, took me, and pulled me off of the bike."

"I'm so sorry," I say.

We drive past the old man's house and then get on the freeway. It's not until that point that I let out a sigh of relief.

"It wasn't just that guy on the motorcycle," Ari says.

As the speedometer reaches eighty miles per hour, I feel a wave of relief wash over me.

"What do you mean?" I ask, suddenly regretting that he's sitting in the front seat, even though he's buckled in.

This is very unsafe, but given what happened it's probably for the best. Ari keeps clinging onto my arm.

"We just have one more exit," I say, "then the police station will be right there."

"The guy on the bike wasn't the only one who came to visit me." The boy repeats himself.

I turn to look at him.

"He was with someone else?"

"Yes, there was somebody. I didn't see him, but he had a loud voice and he yelled at him, and the man on the motorcycle was scared."

"What are you talking about?"

"He kept telling him to kill me. He kept telling him that he was stupid, and he was calling him mean names. He was saying all sorts of words that Mommy said were bad."

"What did he want him to do?"

"He said that I raised you better than this. That you can't leave witnesses. What's a witness?" Ari asks.

I stare at him. Holy crap. There's somebody else involved in this.

"He said he made mistakes and that he can't keep anyone alive. I didn't understand what he was saying. He was yelling a lot. I thought he was going to hurt me and the man on the motorcycle. When I saw him the next time, he was sad. When I asked him why, he said that his daddy yelled at him."

My mouth drops open.

"He said his daddy yelled at him?" I ask.

The boy nods and then closes his eyes.

"I'm tired now," he says, and I let him drift off to sleep just as we pull up to the station.

37

CHARLOTTE

When Dylan comes home from the hospital, I am home to get him comfortable. I got a few more days off and, though he does need my help, I can feel myself getting antsy. Every day he seems to be getting stronger but then something happens and he has a few bad days. He doesn't sleep well and gets into a dark mood. I try to cheer him up, but nothing I do seems to help. Instead, he asks me to give him some space.

Kelsey and I have been texting each other back and forth ever since we had that conversation about my father and I reach out to her like before. But this time I call. I try to be upbeat but she can tell that something is wrong. I keep it to myself at first but she doesn't let up. Finally, I tell her about Dylan. She listens patiently before taking a deep breath.

"You need to cut him some slack. He has been through a lot. You have no idea how much he's struggling with survivor's guilt and anger at his partner and how much he's kicking himself for not helping him more."

"There was nothing he could really do," I insist.

"It doesn't matter. Dylan is recovering. He is trying to make the best of it but there are going to be setbacks. This isn't a linear process."

"What is?"

"Acceptance of what has happened."

Now, it's my turn to pause. I know that she's partly talking about herself and everything that has happened in her life. I wait for her to say that you of all people should know what it's like to live with regret, but she doesn't. She's too much of a good person for that.

"I'm sorry, Kelsey." The words escape my lips. "I'm sorry for everything that I did and didn't do."

"I know and you don't have to be. You were a stupid teenager who was just trying not to get in trouble."

"I should have known better. I should have come to find you sooner."

"Perhaps, but life happens as it happens, Charlotte. We make mistakes, we learn from them. You're a different person now than you were back then. You found me and you made me believe that I wasn't crazy. That is enough."

I find it hard to believe, but I don't really have another choice.

"Listen, I was thinking about something and I hope that you can help me," Kelsey says after a long pause.

She is banging something around in her kitchen and then the humdrum noise of a knife hitting the cutting board as she chops vegetables.

"Sure, anything," I say.

"I keep wondering why my DNA wasn't a match to my parents when we are both certain that I'm the real Kelsey Hall. One possibility is that there was some sort of mistake at the DNA laboratory, right?"

"Uh-huh," I mumble.

"But my parents were so certain that it wasn't me. Like they didn't even want to consider it. Why?"

"They did have one person who tried to extort them for money, pretending to know about your whereabouts," I say.

"Yes, of course. But what if it was something else?"

"Like what?"

"What if they knew that the DNA would not match?"

"What are you talking about?"

"Like what if they adopted me and they didn't want me to know? Then the DNA would definitely not match. Right?"

I think about that for a moment. But something doesn't make sense.

"Wait, but why would they get the DNA test in the first place if they knew that it wouldn't match?" I ask.

"I don't know. Maybe the cops insisted on it. Maybe they didn't want to come out and say anything. But this is a possibility, right?" she asks.

I nod and clear my throat. "Yes, it's definitely an option. But that would mean that they didn't really want to…"

I let my words trail off. There's a pause on the other end.

"Yes, it would mean that they didn't really want to find me. If they knew that they adopted me and they knew that my DNA wouldn't match theirs and they wanted to find me, they would tell the police that. They would probably try to find my biological parents and get my real DNA so that they would have that to go on. But they didn't."

I let her words hang in the air for a minute, processing it all. Clearly, this is something that she has been thinking about for some time because she isn't one bit surprised by the revelation. But for me, it's a bit to process. I was still under the impression that there was a mistake made in the lab and that I would have to go to Seattle and fight against the grain to figure it out. I had briefly entertained this other possibility of adoption, but now it seems like the most likely one.

"Are you there?" Kelsey asks after a moment.

"Yes, I am. What can I do to help you find out the truth?" I offer when I get ahold of myself.

"I can get my DNA profile and do that whole ancestry thing, and maybe I should anyway. But I was wondering if you'd be willing to just go to Seattle to their house with me? I want to knock on their door and see them in person. I know that they'll recognize me, but I want you there for support in case they say I'm not her."

"Of course," I say without even taking a moment to think about it.

"Really? Are you sure?"

"It's the least I can do," I say.

"Thank you. You have no idea what this means to me. This month is busy but maybe next month, okay? Let's plan the trip."

IN THE NEXT FEW DAYS, the story behind Keith Moraine's father starts to unravel. When I run the license plate on the Jeep outside the mining shaft, I discover that it is registered to a man named David Paul Perpich. When I show his driver's license picture to Ari, he says that he has never seen the man or heard his name. On the surface, he seems to have no connection to Keith Moraine.

We bring Keith's mother in for questioning. This time, I am not handling her with kid gloves. She has already provided us with a lot of information, but I need more answers. Even though she is still angry that I did not live up to my promise of keeping her son safe, she does tell me that she used to be married to a man named Paul Griggs, whom she had not had contact with in years.

"Paul is Keith's father, but as far as I know, he hasn't seen him since he was a toddler," Mrs. Moraine says, staring out into the distance behind me in the interrogation room.

"Did Keith ever ask you about him?"

"Of course. All the time. It was all he ever wanted to talk about as a kid. After a while, I just started to make things up because I couldn't very well tell him the truth."

"And that is?"

"That I left Paul in the middle of the night because I was worried that he would kill both of us."

"So, he was abusive?" I ask.

"He would come home from his business trips and anything and everything would set him off. Kids are hard but kids who cry a lot are the hardest. Keith was like that and Paul couldn't handle it. He would go into a rage and smack both of us around. One time, he pushed the TV on top of me and broke my arm. Another time, he bloodied up my eyes so badly, I couldn't see for weeks."

"So, you decided to leave him?"

"Yeah, the day before he was supposed to come back from another trip, I took off. Keith was three at the time. I packed up what I could and we lived in my car for months, looking over our shoulder all the time."

When the lieutenant knocks on the door, I step out for a moment.

"CSI went through Keith's laptop and found recent photographs of him and his father. After further investigation, they confirmed that David Paul Perpich, the owner of the Jeep, is Paul Griggs."

"So, Ari was right. His dad was there all along telling him to do these things," I say. "Even though he didn't recognize him when I showed him his picture."

"The dad might not have actually been there or showed his face to Ari. Now, let's not forget that Keith's an adult who kidnapped and murdered and had full agency in everything he had done despite his father. But this information does shed light on the broader version of the story."

"How did they get in touch after all of those years?" I ask.

"Keith was searching for him for a while. Paul had changed his name and he wasn't an easy person to find. There is a stack of emails that you still need to go through to piece everything together, but CSI said that he found a friend of a friend of a friend who happened to know his whereabouts. He then reached out to him on social media and asked if he had a son named Keith. After that, they emailed and called each other all the time."

The lieutenant sighs and takes a few big gulps of his soda.

"Any ideas about his whereabouts?" I ask.

"The phone number is obviously dead. But we do have an APB out. Paul has a lot of experience changing names and disappearing. There are no other vehicles registered to him and we gave his name to airlines, railroads, and bus depots, but who knows. If he has other identification, he might escape."

The headache that was hardly noticeable a few minutes ago is starting to pound so loudly that it's hard to hear. Keith, the man responsible for the deaths of the two boys and the kidnapping of the last one, is dead but the last piece of the puzzle is unsolved.

What exactly was Paul's involvement in those murders?

What happens if he disappears into the vastness of the West?

Will we ever catch him?

The door at the end of the hallway swings open. FBI agent Philip Welch walks toward the lieutenant and me in his usual earnest Boy Scout manner.

He flashes me a smile and says, "I'd like to thank you both for taking me in and making me feel so comfortable in Mesquite County. It has been a total pleasure to work with everyone."

"Of course," the lieutenant says. "I can't tell you how much we appreciate having the FBI here and all of your resources."

I clench my jaw. The FBI didn't solve this case. The FBI didn't go looking for the kid in the mineshaft. I did.

But it's not the FBI that I'm really mad at, it's Philip. The phone that he dunked in the water couldn't be revived, destroying evidence of all of his criminality. I have no proof of what he had done to me, but my resolve to expose him has gotten stronger.

"I guess we'll take things over from here," Philip says, extending his hand to me. "Paul Griggs is on the run across state lines and he has to be found and prosecuted. That's what we do best."

I leave his hand in the air without meeting it with mine until the lieutenant notices and shakes it, giving me a glare. He doesn't know the details of what happened all those years ago. No one at work does, except Will.

But maybe it's time to change that.

THANK you for reading Missing Lives. I hope you have enjoyed it. Want to know what happens next? 1-click GIRL IN THE LAKE now!

Hidden secrets and deadly lies...

Following the incident that nearly killed her boyfriend, **Detective Charlotte Pierce needs a weekend away** with him in the quaint **mountain town of Quail Lake, California.**

However, their trip is interrupted **when a sixteen-year-old camp counselor goes missing. The girl's body** is later found by the lake shore **with strangulation marks** around her neck and bruises all over.

1-click GIRL IN THE LAKE now!

CAN'T GET ENOUGH? Read LAKE OF LIES (A Detective Charlotte Pierce novella) for FREE!

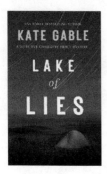

SPECIAL REQUEST: Please make sure to take a moment to leave a review on the retailer of your choice. Reviews really help me find more readers.

IF YOU FIND any issues or mistakes, please feel free to reach out to me directly at Kate@kategable.com

THANK YOU!

BE THE FIRST TO KNOW ABOUT MY UPCOMING SALES, NEW RELEASES AND EXCLUSIVE GIVEAWAYS!

Want a Free book? Sign up for my Newsletter!

Sign up for my newsletter:

https://www.subscribepage.com/kategableviplist

Join my Facebook Group:
https://www.facebook.com/groups/833851020557518

Bonus Points: Follow me on BookBub and
Goodreads!

https://www.goodreads.com/author/show/21534224.
Kate_Gable

ABOUT KATE GABLE

Kate Gable loves a good mystery that is full of suspense. She grew up devouring psychological thrillers and crime novels as well as movies, tv shows and true crime.

Her favorite stories are the ones that are centered on families with lots of secrets and lies as well as many twists and turns. Her novels have elements of psychological suspense, thriller, mystery and romance.

Kate Gable lives near Palm Springs, CA with her husband, son, a dog and a cat. She has spent more than twenty years in Southern California and finds inspiration from its cities, canyons, deserts, and small mountain towns.

She graduated from University of Southern California with a Bachelor's degree in Mathematics. After pursuing graduate studies in mathematics, she switched gears and got her MA in Creative Writing and English from Western New Mexico University and her PhD in Education from Old Dominion University.

Writing has always been her passion and obsession. Kate is also a USA Today Bestselling author of romantic suspense under another pen name.

Write her here:

Kate@kategable.com

Check out her books here:

www.kategable.com

Sign up for my newsletter:
https://www.subscribepage.com/kategableviplist

Join my Facebook Group:
https://www.facebook.com/groups/833851020557518

Bonus Points: Follow me on BookBub and Goodreads!

https://www.bookbub.com/authors/kate-gable

https://www.goodreads.com/author/show/21534224.
Kate_Gable

ALSO BY KATE GABLE

All books are available at ALL major retailers! If you can't find it, please email me at
kate@kategable.com
www.kategable.com

Detective Kaitlyn Carr

Girl Missing (Book 1)
Girl Lost (Book 2)
Girl Found (Book 3)
Girl Taken (Book 4)
Girl Forgotten (Book 5)

Girl Hidden (FREE Novella)

Detective Charlotte Pierce

Last Breath
Nameless Girl
Missing Lives
Girl in the Lake

Lake of Lies (FREE Novella)

Made in the USA
Middletown, DE
19 February 2024

50032101R00186